FOK, The American Dream!

By: Lory Mentor

FOK The American Dream!

Published by Lory Mentor in Partnership with
The Writer's Drive Thru

Manufactured in the United States of America

ISBN #: 978-1-950279-28-9

Dedication

To my parents and every immigrant's parents who sacrifice their dreams, their freedom and their lives so their children can have a better life. I thank you and I am forever grateful.

FOK The American Dream!

Acknowledgements

I want to take a moment to thank my creator the God of all gods for allowing me to be one of his vessels and inspiring me to create great literature for this Era.

FOK The American Dream!

The Reasons Immigrants Migrate to America.

It is very interesting how Americans, Black and White Americans, see White and Black immigrants as a threat. They see us as intruders who should not be here. But, I wonder if they ever try to find out why we are really here? Why did we leave all that we knew to come to a foreign land? I just wonder if they ever think of those deeper questions or even try to understand our journey to the land of the free.

Yes, the land of the FREE! Let's talk, Americans. I mean, who would not run to the land of the "FREE" if they were being persecuted because of their religion? Let's think, who would not? I was told in US history that's why the Pilgrims came to America the LAND of the FREE. So, DON'T YOU THINK IT makes perfect sense for other immigrants to run, swim, or fly to AMERICA the Land of the FREE so they can worship and pray to their God peacefully and Freely. Your forefathers did it, well you know the white Europeans, the ones who fled Europe to come to America. So why can't we do it too?

Technically, only the Natives of America can have a say in the subject of immigrants like myself and your grandparents coming to America. Just like the Europeans came here on boats to be able to save their lives and practice their religion freely. I know many immigrants from the Middle East who had to pay to come to America in order to save their lives and be able to worship their God. That's the beauty of America my fellow Americans; that all of us who are immigrants and descendants of immigrants can live alongside each other and practice our own religion in peace.

Now we all know that not every country in the world oppressed their inhabitants and forced them to practice one religion. So, what other reasons can immigrants come here? Let's take a minute to think! What about politics? Can you even imagine after voting for a politician the other party comes to your house and kills your entire family?

Yeah, it is that real! I know people who were in my ESL class who went through that at an early age. Matter of fact, many people from Latin America came here for that reason. I know a lot of people from Central America, West Africa, East Africa, and people from Asia who fled here because they had political differences. When I think about it, I remember reading in history books that The American Government welcomed Jewish individuals with open arms when they were oppressed by Hitler. Even if it was not right away but they did, but it is very different when it comes to other group of immigrants

Wait, what was the reason America was founded? I remember learning how the Revolutionary War started because a group of individuals that Americans call their forefathers were against the British political views. Well, they didn't want to keep paying tax to England so they defended their beliefs and that's how America was founded with 13 colonies. But before I go any further, I'll tell you something personal. Why my family left the land that we love to come to the land of the free.

I know some neighbors who left China because they could not voice their opinion about their government. They are not even allowed to have as many kids that they want. My classmates told me their family immigrated here because his parents had him. Americans don't even like putting their dogs to sleep; can you even imagine putting your newborn child to sleep?

Just like many immigrants who left their country for political reasons, I also fled my island that I love for those reasons. I share my story to many immigrants from other parts of the world and I meet people who have similar stories as myself. Isn't it wonderful that we live in a country that we can get up and vote for a politician and go home and watch *Wendy! How you doing?* without caring? That's the beauty of liberty!

Well in my case, in my country when I was just a child things were different. I remember when a popular violent politician came into power in the 1990's. I was only a child but some experiences you go through in life stick with you. My childhood was great. I lived in a bourgeois city. My parents came from two different social classes and two different cities. My mom came from a wealthy family and she was a teacher who became a housewife after she got married. My dad was self-made, who used to work for the United Nations as a librarian. It's pretty clear that I grew up in an intellectual family. My siblings and I went to private schools and took etiquette lessons on the weekends, so you see life was pretty amazing.

That is until this politician was elected. I would rather not state his name so his children can live in peace. However, he started preaching violence to the ones who were oppressed. The ones who were poor were in survival mode, so they were going to people's homes demanding what they didn't have. They also wanted everyone who worked for the UN to be out of the country. We were a threat; my father worked for the UN, wore his uniform proudly daily, and he was a researcher at the UN library. He helped a lot of college students and that was a big no. Just like the slave master, the politician didn't want the mass population to be educated. So, the country was a mess!

I still remember the first day that president came back from exile, people were chanting for him. He made the announcement to go after anyone who was against him and our family's life was in danger. I remember that morning I woke up and my father didn't come home. There were people outside our gate trying to get in. My siblings and I had to hide under the beds, and we couldn't make one sound. Our nanny told us do not even sneeze or all of us are dead!

She crawled to the kitchen to get pieces of bread to eat. We had to crawl to go use the bathroom, but we could not flush the toilet. The guys could not get in, but they patrolled outside our gates for five days.

We spent five days laying on the cold floor. On the fifth day when a couple of guys jumped the fence, I prayed silently in my heart   they didn't see anyone one of us. They looked inside our windows and said, "They probably left, let's go." That very day at the age of 8, I asked God to forgive my sins and I took off my jewelry just in case; I was ready to die. But, God was with us! God protected us! God made those men walk away and not enter our house.

But, those same guys entered our neighbors' homes and we heard gunshots. I never saw some of my neighbors, my childhood friends, again. As for us, we were able to survive a political civil war. And, we saw my father weeks later. He was stuck in the UN base for the entire week. Every time he called us; we didn't pick up the phone because we were afraid for our lives. We left that neighborhood that same month and lived in an isolated area in the city.

One evening as we were walking in our new neighborhood full of woods, that same political party tried to kidnap my siblings and I after school. I was 9 at that time and we were not allowed to go outside by ourselves after that. That was my reality as a child growing up in a political conflict. Thankfully 2 years later we came to America, the land of liberty. The land of the free and the land of justice for all.

I just want to ask a question or two to my fellow Americans who believe in freedom. What would you do as a parent? What would you do as a human being? We left because we could afford to leave. Just in case you were wondering how we entered this lovely country; it was with money. We traveled on American Airlines! We paid for every visit to the embassy. We paid for our Green Card. After we entered this country, we continued to pay for our green card every time it expired. Yes, money brought us our freedom. Money allowed us to come to the land of the free. We have to pay for a lifetime, and if we choose to become American citizens we have to pay and take a test. I took my test while I was in college.

Matter of fact, I know this older lady who has been in this country for over 30 years. She didn't know how to read or write in her native tongue. Growing up in the 40s, women weren't allowed to go to school in her country, so she never sat one day in a classroom. She didn't pass the test because she couldn't spell shoes, and at the age of 72-years-old she lost her money, and her chance to be an American. I am just stating some facts just in case you didn't know anything about your immigration laws.

One other popular reason immigrants come here is because they are starving. They can't find jobs in their native lands. I have a lot of friends who left their country for that reason and it is the same reason a lot of the so-called forefathers of America came here. We all know that Europe can't produce much, so a lot of Europeans left to come live in America; the land of milk and honey.

For some reason now it is more of an issue for us immigrants to come and prosper like everyone did in the past. Immigration laws are getting more strict and now allegedly a wall is in construction. I guess

America is no longer the land of the free. Now I wonder what America is. I have realized that America has been dealing with a lot of issues that don't really concern us immigrants. But, since we are the outsider it makes perfect sense to blame every issue on us immigrants who have no business in American politics. I pray that Americans may find peace and learn to love one another and also find God. May the God who blesses America touch the people's hearts so they can comprehend that they are equal in the eyes of God their maker, the God of unity and love.

I do love America, we have this relationship, this bond. No matter how long I am away from this beautiful massive land, when I return it is nothing but love until I overstay my visit. At the end of the day, I understand that most Americans don't understand the importance of hospitality. I can't be mad at someone because there are certain things they didn't learn growing up. Their parents had no other choice but to work and pay bills so that their children can have the necessities of life. But in the midst of their sacrifice, some parents didn't have the opportunity to teach their children the essence of life or how to be an authentic human being.

I do want the best for America and for its people to strive and have time to enjoy life a little. Even though my mom did sacrifice her whole being for me to be here in America and I am forever thankful for that, I did benefit from this land. I did learn how to be this great human being that I am today. Thanks to America I have my PhD and I am proud to say that I am the product of two beautiful countries that I love dearly. But, now it is my time as an immigrant to leave the land and go back to my native lands so the true Americans, the indigenous people, can enjoy their land.

When immigrants were insulted, persecuted, or needed refuge from their native land, they ran to America. But now when those same immigrants and their children are persecuted, insulted, or just need a peace of mind so they can be their best selves, what must we do? It is pretty scary to leave, but what if the Land of the Free doesn't feel like it is the land of the free to certain groups of people? Or if liberty for all does not address you or your people, what must you do? It's scary for some undocumented immigrants to live on this land right now.

We know what happens when we fight hate with hate, nothing positive comes from that. So, if we as immigrants choose to stay, are we then constantly fighting a spiritual war? We could be growing spiritually with peace and harmony in another environment where we are wanted and appreciated. It is a new era "Spiritualism", which means spiritual awakening! Where every human being becomes more aware that we are a spiritual being living in a human body. Because of this awareness we are now seeking for the reason of our existence and who created us. Why are we here on earth? What is our purpose? Meanwhile, we are deeply seeking to understand self and connecting to our higher being our creator.

Finding our purpose is way more important than fighting for a piece of land that we will be buried under many centuries to come. Isn't life more precious than America? Who sells immigrants a dream of liberty and freedom so we can run to America when we are being persecuted in our own homeland. And, once we understand the American system we quickly find out the reality, that it is all a masquerade.

Since love keeps no record of wrong, I will say that God bless the American people, the Black and White Americans who have been fighting hand in hand to make sure that America is the land of the free for all. Fight your good fight and may the Lord of peace be with you. While I, an immigrant, I choose to be a pioneer and go back to my native land So I can dive into spiritualism, as the wave of freedom liberates my Awaken body, as I sip in success blend in with cold cash in the shores of Ayiti!

Remember my fellow immigrants to share your story. Our voice must be heard! so others can be liberated. See you next time. And don't forget to comment below and share your story. May Peace and love be with you all.

FOK The American Dream!

The Unrevealed Immigrant Experience

Louverture and Dessalines are both sitting in the front porch watching the blogger express herself on a phone screen. They are both amazed to hear A young immigrant like themselves who is able to tell her truth fearlessly and unapologetically to millions of viewers.

Both Louverture and Dessalines share similar experiences with the blogger. They also know many immigrants who can't voice their truth like the blogger. After they watch her video it sparks a conversation, around their personal experiences and their loved one's personal experiences in America.

FOK The American Dream!

Scene 1

Louverture- (looking at the screen of the phone and shaking his head) Are you serious, do you now see why I always say, "Fuck the American dream man", This blogger talk so boldly about a lot of facts that Americans seems to ignore or has no clue on what we go through. God bless her for starting this conversation.

Dessalines- Yes I am amaze right now. What she said resonated with me on so many levels.

Louverture- Me too, she truly gave me the confirmation that America is not our home and us immigrants were never living for ourselves but for the greater good of the American Society. I can't live like this anymore, I cannot be worrying about making a country great, great again to be exact when I need to focus on being great. (point at self) I have to live my dreams and make things happen for me. (raise his voice) I have one life to live so it's all about me, myself, and I. I am a dreamer! I have a dream! Trust and believe all my dreams will come true!

Dessalines - I definitely understand your frustration. I face them every day just like you, but you need to tone your voice down. You're an immigrant, plus you're Black with an accent and you cannot be screaming like that..

Louverture- (speak softly) I am sorry I don't want to disrespect your mother's home and draw the wrong attention. But because I am black with an accent it gives me the right to express myself.

Marcus Garvey was from Jamaica, he expressed himself freely so why can't I. Cesar Chaves was from Mexico another immigrant, who stood up for the immigrant workers and made sure all immigrants received a green card and equal pay. It is because of Chaves my mother received her green card. I am a warrior just like them. I too have a voice; I too have a legacy to leave behind for the next generation.

Dessalines - Yeah I definitely understand you and agree with you. It is because of Chaves my mother got her green card too; but you need to relax. The police are cleaning the streets in the hood right now especially with us immigrants!

Louverture- I am highly protected and highly blessed! We are surrounded by God's angels! Not a string of hair can be removed from my head. You see how Dick Gregory was untouchable? We are divinely protected. My creator loves me, plus we are Haitian. You don't recall how we shook the Brooklyn bridge when the FDA was trying to spread false rumors about us. You see our last name. We are a high breed plus you know!

Dessalines - I know, I know but we are not on our own land, ICE is going around deporting people left to right, trust me I saw it with my own two eyes. Do you remember Abebe, the African man who lived two doors down from me.

Louverture- Yea I remember him; He is Muslim right. (shake his head) Oh yes I remember him. He was always speaking French to you trying to get me jealous or something.

Dessalines- really, cut that out, he is a married man and you know that too, well you know he got deported right.

Louverture- what? how? That man had 3 jobs; the only time we saw him was when he was going to work or coming back from work. What happened?

Dessalines - Yeah he was flourishing too, but he got caught with a box cutter. All Abebe did was work, he would leave his home at 5 am and come home at 12 am almost every day. Sometimes he would even work overnight at the group home he has been working at since he first came to America.

Louverture- yes I remember, When I used to live here, I used to see him leaving his home before the sun rose in the morning..

Dessalines- Well, one day he was coming from work from the warehouse after 12 am, and you know how Devran's little brother and his friends are always playing music on their porch extra loud in the summer. So Nosey Nancy called the cops, so Devan turned off the music and everyone ran inside to hide. But poor Abebe minding his own business saw the cop's car and continued walking like he didn't know the street codes. I always told Abebe American cops are not Africa cops; and not every cop has respect for us because we work and pay taxes. Some cops are not properly trained, They are scared every time they come to the hood, they are in survival mode.

Louverture- yea, how can they protect us if they think we are their enemy?

Dessalines- Exactly! And that's how I explained it to him too, but noooo he didn't believe me. His theory was he is a positive influence to the American society. He pays taxes like everyone else. The police are here to protect all of us good citizens.

Louverture- technically Abebe is right, that is the police job description, they are here to protect and serve all. But we know

Dessalines- Oh yes we know; evidently Abebe knew also when the police stopped him that night. Abebe had both of his hands in the air when they stopped him. They search him and saw he had a praying bead in his pocket so they ask Abebe if he had a gun on him since he is Muslim. I guess they assume all Muslims are terrorists. They threw him on the ground while this one cop had his foot on Abebe's head like he was an animal. Once they saw the box cutter in his backpack they took him to the precinct. The next day they sent him to the county jail. Once he saw a judge they saw his record was clean but his visa was expired; you know what the judge said to him?

Louverture-Deportation.

Dessalines- yup, But you know what disturbs me? Abebe country doesn't take deportees; they will kill anyone who gets deported, that's the law of his country, so the US. the government has no other choice to keep him here and treat him like an American. You know, have him serve his time or probation, after that give him proper documents so he can function in the American society. But instead of releasing Abebe they had him sitting in prison for

90 days for their financial gain, well you know how it is?

Louverture- Oh yes that is why I am done with that lifestyle, when I thought I was a big-time hustler hustling the streets God made me realize the system was hustling me. Every time I served a sentence they were making money off me. Can you believe I thought I was winning back then when in reality I was losing both at life and myself. Thank God for real.

Dessalines- Oh yes, I am so happy for you now, This system is so unfair. Instead of paying for students loans and paying for people to go to College they are building prison. That tells a lot about how this society views its nation. Even if they gave Abebe his papers he would have lost all 3 jobs because he had a charge and they said he was resisting arrest.

Louverture - Are you serious?

Dessalines- Yes I am, I saw Abebe that night from my kitchen window, When the cops stopped him he had both hands up, before the cop car parked. That's probably why they didn't kill him. But instead of allowing him to stay in this country and give him his papers, they told Abebe to choose another country in Africa to go to. So, he had to go to a country where he doesn't speak the language or know anyone.

Louverture- Wow this is happening in American soil? That's a shame

Dessalines- And What if they did that to Americans? They would be tormented, but they do it to immigrants. Thanks to God things went well for him. Abebe told me that immigration is like the slave ship back in the days. They have everyone in one big plane on the floor with chains on their ankle and wrist and shipping them to different locations. Can you believe this?

Louverture- I believe you. Matter of fact, I know this young man who's from Guadeloupe and ended up in Haiti after he was deported from the United States. Things like this happen every day that's why I started thinking of leaving this artificial freedom this country has to offer. But since we are on the camel's back, we can't talk too much about his back being a hump. We can only be grateful for the unpleasant ride that is taking us to our destination.

Dessalines- I definitely see what you mean when you say Fuck the American dream. When you take a good look at it, what type of dream is that? Can someone please define it for me?

Louverture- the worst thing about this, who is going to speak for someone like Abebe? This dossier will not even make the 12 o'clock news. He is a Black immigrant with an accent. Abebe might as well go live in his country and be at peace, not when I heard he has a mansion in his country with a sexy beautiful wife.

Dessalines - Yes he does, actually he has four mansions with acres of land and a swimming pool on each property and anything else you can think of. His estates are way bigger than Beyoncé's for real. Abebe always looked poor every time I used to see him but Abebe's a smart man. Plus, he has a wife who is loyal, business minded who handled all his businesses in his country for him. They rent 3 of

24

the homes to millionaires and the wife stays in another with 2 of their kids, and his mom has her own estate too. That's the first home he had built when he came to America 7 years ago. Plus, his wife has clothing stores in 4 different countries in Africa. Not some regular boutiques she has warehouses, So you know it's top-notch. Plus, she has great hair connections. She is the main hair supplier in her country. If you go on her IG you will see what I'm talking about. They have nice cars too, foreign cars only.

Louverture- (looking at her Instagram account through his phone) wow that's inspiration right there. Abebe hasn't been in the U.S for a long time and he is already a billionaire. That's a true hustler for real. He has worked hard, made his clean money that will continue to grow. That's a great couple, you know his capital will augment for many generations, and he is blessed with a great wife.

Dessalines- She is a sweetheart, a God-fearing woman. I called Abebe's wife right after they took him to the precinct. You know what she told me? Allah had answered her prayers! Good, it's time for her man to come home. She told me to tell her king to pick Ghana as the country he would like to be deported to since she has businesses there she knows her way around. When he gets to Ghana, she will pick him up from their private jet and take him home.

Louverture- A private jet wow, I have nothing but respect for that man. That's what I was telling you last week. They want us immigrants to leave, then let's just leave what do you think? This could be you and me.

Dessalines- I don't know about all of that, God has bless Abebe with a great wife

Louverture-. Abebe better listen to his wife too because this country doesn't have any love for people like him. To tell you the truth, it's illegal to deport someone to another country when their own country doesn't accept deportees. The right thing they should do is give him his legal papers and let him stay in the country. That's what they do to the Cubans, so why can't they do it to this African king?

Dessalines- that is true But God had other plans for him. Abebe has more than enough at home anyways, but my heart goes out to the ones who actually don't have anybody or speak the language. What are they going to do when they get to a foreign country? That's cruel.

Louverture- Always remember there is a God who will always make a way for us out of no way out. Imagine if we left this country and go live in our own country just like the blogger we were just watching on your phone, just imagine the things you and I can accomplish

Dessalines- But we can't leave like that, you and one of your girls need to have a plan. Imagine if every immigrant left this place what would happen to America?

Louverture- You know I do not have a girlfriend, but it is okay.

Dessalines- okay if you say so, Anyways just like the blogger mentioned earlier I also believe it's a new era approaching. "Spiritualism" is on the rise.

Louverture- I agree, lots of people are waking up and being aware of the spirit within that is their true essence.

Dessalines- But, I see people all over the internet mentioning they are woke. Sometimes I feel like writing under their post, relax you're not woke you are waking up! Please stop acting like you're the guru for social media. Unless you can answer these deeper questions of; who you are? Why are you here? Who created you? What's your purpose? And other deep questions that has to do with the inner man, the spirit within..

Louverture- I am still finding answers to those questions myself, but collectively I feel that us the human race we are finally on the right track learning and being aware of the importance of life in general. That's why us the Millennials we are seeking for more, going beyond the limits and controlling our own destiny

Dessalines- That is true, we have to start somewhere. You know I always wonder how things will be if I quit my job and become an entrepreneur in my own land, But after I saw how the blogger is relaxing at her beach house makes me want to pursue this life of freedom. I think you are right we need to leave this country. Maybe not together but I feel like I need to leave and go somewhere I am profitable so I can prosper in peace. Because sometimes I feel like every day is a treat in the media, making statements about immigrants that are

90% of the time incorrect. Someone in my office called me an immigrant the other day, too. So, you know circumstances just got real for us immigrants.

Louverture- Really, but don't let that bother you, if that person knew better they will never say anything to offend you. That person is probably in lack, jealous because you are their boss with a thick accent and he desires that position. So, at the end he is only blocking his goods. To tell you the truth, jealousy is only being afraid of losing something that you don't have.

Dessalines- You right, this whole time I was focusing on the fact that Americans don't know a thing about their own immigration system, but this entire time he was just upset because he felt like I am the cause of him losing the position he hoped for.

Louverture- Yea that's how I look at things now, I made the decision to not take anything personal anymore. That's what helps me find my true calling, But it is also very important to know the law of your land for fact.

Dessalines - Imagine if all Americans knew how much money immigrants bring in this country they would have appreciated us more. One example out of many is my cousin, you know who the one who came to visit weeks before the earthquakes took place in Haiti.

Louverture- (nodding his head) Yes I remember her.

Dessalines- She was not planning on staying in America but she had no other choice because she lost all that she had in Haiti. Now she has some form of paperwork called TPS papers. Come to find out she has to pay almost $600 every 2 years, plus she pays for a working card. And every time she wants to travel outside of the country she pay immigration $300 dollars so they can give her access to leave the country, plus she also has to pay for her ticket.. Now you see how much revenue they are making from each person with a TPS statue? There are billions of people with TPS in this country, so you know America is flourishing!

Louverture- Wow I didn't even know that, that is why I do not blame immigrants who come to America, work hard, save their money and go back to their country with all of it. I had this Mexican co-worker at my job when I was working my but off at the restaurant to start my businesses.

Dessalines- Oh yea I remember him, it used to be you in him slaving in the kitchen day in night. He used to make sure to give me extra food when you and him used to work there.

Louverture- You would not believe what he told me.

Dessalines What?

Louverture- He told me he came to this country with the same truck that brings in the drugs. He told me that's the safest way to come into America. He said they never check those trucks at all. Matter of fact, the US borders are not allowed to touch certain trucks and the truck he was in is one of them.

Dessalines- what? He was probably lying.

Louverture- I don't know but if he was lying but this drug trafficking, it's a vicious business that is destroying America's youth. In the 80s it was affecting the hood and almost every Black American's parents were addicted to this poison. Statistics have shown this diabolical business is destroying the kids in the suburbs now. The young White kids are dying at a rapid rate from opioids or other drugs in the nation. Pedro told me as long as these trucks keep coming in the immigrants will come in too. It's the two best ways to keep American economy up, the immigrants and the drug trade.

Dessalines- I don't know if Pedro was telling me the truth but that will be irrational if the drugs and the immigrants were coming in the same truck and knew all about it but can't touch the trucks to put an end to this disease; But they are putting in prison little distributors in the ghetto when they know the source to their war on drug bullshit. But anyways, I'm glad my brothers aren't doing that type of demoralized hustle anymore. They are following Nipsey Hussle footsteps in order to find their true path out of this degrading lifestyle.

Louverture- I am so thankful that I was able to get out of this brutal cycle just like Nip did. Now one has time for this deadly lifestyle. Everyone is aiming toward the life of positivity and spiritually, we all want to change like Nip did. And you know what, I just realized they didn't kill Nip, they killed the desires of being in a gang to young kids growing up in the ghetto. This gang just died in that same city it was popular in. Plus, it was Nipsey's time to go to his maker, he had accomplished his mission on earth.

Dessalines- That is true, plus why join a set of negative mindsets when they don't want you to be great?

Louverture- Exactly! Nipsey manifested himself out of all the negative situations. He created 7 principles for people like him who want a better life to follow. He bought his block, created jobs for his people, and created generational wealth. His family will be comfortable for life.

Dessalines- You're right about that. His whole family will always be financially independent. Plus, he did what he came to do on this earth. He lived his full purpose; how many people can say that? His name will be in history books right next to Rev. Dr. Martin Luther King Jr., Harriet Tubman, and every human being who wanted better for their community and for themselves. Plus, his block that he bought is named after him. That's a king from above who came to earth and lived his full potential and left a blueprint for everyone to follow, just like Harriet Tubman freed thousands of slaves. That's the type of man I like.

Louverture- You are right, because when I look around this neighborhood all I see is young men in the hood working 2 jobs and saving their money to open businesses. Within 6 month to a year everyone in the hood is shopping from their businesses. It is really a new era, Young men and women are stepping up and becoming great influencers in their community.

Dessalines- Oh yes I see that all the time; Pretty soon all these county jails and prisons are going to be rehabs like my sociology professor told me years ago. Some juvenile facilities are already rehab centers. Its spiritualism for real, things are happening without even a fight.

Louverture - I agree, multitudes of men are coming home, and they are changing their narratives. They are doing positive things like working and opening businesses. I see true gangsters coming home, making honest money, and the so-called psychologists can't even understand what is happening.

Dessalines- It's spiritualism for sure.

Louverture- Our creator heard our cries, he sees our hearts, and now he is helping us. I believe in the higher force and he is on the innocent's side for sure. Just like he helped us get out of slavery but this time it's different, it's greater. Ex inmates like myself are coming home with an abundance of knowledge and understanding, So we know how to really connect to the higher being our creator.

Dessalines - Yeah I do see a lot of people changing their mind set, like Biggie said, "I went from negative to positive and it is all good."

Louverture- Plus God is blessing us with knowledge like king Solomon and we are utilizing every bit of that knowledge and understanding.

Dessalines- Indeed, we are wise. us millennials are making a change that is unheard of. Society does not understand us; they say we are not reliable because we want to live to our highest calling instead of staying at a job for 55 years. We are risking it all and living our best life while living our calling.

Louverture- That is so true, my manager at the restaurant I used to work at still cannot understand how Pedro left the restaurant to move back to his country, and six month later I left and started my own business. I was always thankful for my job at the restaurant but I had a vision, Pedro had a vision and I believe every millennials have their own vision they are manifesting into reality.

Dessalines- By the way, you still haven't told me what happened to Pedro. He was a walking intellect like you. Pedro was the first person who told me how his ancestors in Mexico had relatives in the Caribbean and in the US. He even told me how not every black person came from Africa on a slave boat, and not every native Indian looks like the ones they have in those reserve camps. We used to talk for hours about stuff like this. But anyways, what happened to Pedro?

Louverture- oh yea Pedro, my Mexican brother. All we did in that restaurant kitchen was exchange knowledge while we flip burgers and make tacos. I never met anyone like Pedro for real, he sacrificed everything to come to America! Even his entire family.

Dessalines -What do you mean his entire family? He was all about family. He used to always talk about the importance of family and unity. How God put us together for a reason and how we are a blessing to one another, how we should remain connected. Now you're telling me he sacrificed his entire family? Wow Pedro was a savage?

Louverture- No, no it didn't happen like that. His family knew about the sacrifice he had to make so he could come to America.

Dessalines - What? really, that's even crazier! I would rather stay in my own country and make something of myself instead of sacrificing my own blood for this fake liberty for all.

Louverture- Don't speak too soon, our parents made sacrifices to come to this country that we will never know or understand.

Dessalines - You right, but to kill your family though?

Louverture- Really who told you that? Those words didn't come out of my mouth. you love to exaggerate things for real.

Dessalines - (laughs) well you're not talking so I'm assuming!

Louverture- Alright, let me tell you the truth Pedro told me. Remember how I told you he came in the same truck that brought in the drugs to the United States?

Dessalines - Yes, I do.

Louverture- Well, in order for him to get on that truck he had to see some people. Before he made the deal, they went to his house and took a picture of his family members including his nieces who were infants. He didn't pay a peso to get in that truck to cross the border, but they gave him 6 months to start making payment. If not they would kill each family member one by one. And his payment was due every first of the month for 2 years. Every time he missed a payment it was at the cost of a family member's life.

Dessalines - Are you serious? He came during the recession before President Obama came in office too.

Louverture- That's a big risk he took for him and his family. You know he had to come with the optimist mentality.

Dessalines- Definitely!

Louverture- like Winston Churchill said, "An optimist sees the opportunity in every difficulty." Some people may not like Trump, but he also said he made the most money during the recession, so you have to learn something from him. I'm telling you Pedro sure did

Dessalines - You're right. You have an optimistic mentality you can make it anywhere in this life. But what happened after Pedro came here? How did he get around and survive?

Louverture- Well when he crossed the border he was 19 years old. He told me that he felt like his entire family was with him. He had 100 dollars in his pocket that he borrowed from a neighbor. The only word he knew was work. His first day instead of staying at his tia's home he decided to sleep under a bridge to save money.

Dessalines - Wait he had an aunt here? Why didn't he want to stay there?

Louverture- No, she is not his aunt. She is just a lady who owns a house. And he will be able to stay there for as long as he can pay her. She is connected to the ones who bring the Mexicans over; it's a clear organized system.

Dessalines - Wow this is like the railroad when the slaves were stopping at different houses until they made their way north. That's why I can't understand why some African Americans get mad at us and tell us to get out of their country. If only they knew that we are going through the same discomfort their ancestors went through; running away from oppression that white supremacy, or the colonizers' children, created in our countries.

Louverture- This world is really a circle; history is repeating itself and we don't even know it.

Dessalines - And if only they knew why so many immigrants come here. Why we make the sacrifices of facing death to come to the land that sells "the ideology of liberty." But once we get here and understand this shady system, we realize this ideology of liberty and unity America sells to other countries in our TV is a lie. It's only a form of manipulation so we can feel like what we have going on in our country is not good enough and we should pack up our bags and come over.

Louverture- Some Americans believe we are only here to take over their land, but the reality is that many Americans are in our country working and living the island dreams. Migrations are happening in both places, but they only want us to know it's only immigrants coming to their lands. That's mind control at its finest.

Dessalines - Of course, but, what happened to Pedro? You keep talking about something else and I need to know what happened to him. He is the first one who told me that most of the natives of Mexico were Black. Matter of fact, both continents of the Americas had Black natives like in the Caribbean. Pedro showed me how we all were one big family before the murderer Christopher Columbus came to our side of the world. And now they want us to believe all of us who are Black came here on the slave trade; the reality is that we were here way before Christopher Columbus.

Louverture- You are right, that is something we do not see in the Western history books. but I remember learning in Haiti history books about the native of Haiti who could have passed as the African slaves. But you keep talking about something else then you're gonna ask me what happened to Pedro?

Dessalines - alright, alright; let's go back to Pedro's story. I'm not going to interrupt anymore. How' he doing?

Louverture- What? you Wendy now (laughs) don't even comment. You better not say one word this time!

(Both are laughing)

Louverture- Before Pedro started working at the restaurant, he used to stand outside and ask for work every single day. Some days he would work and get paid, and other days they would take advantage of him. You know beat him up, spit on his face, or make him work and not pay him.

Dessalines - What? Are you serious?

Toussaint- Oh yes, he experienced all of that. But you know it's already a crime to be an immigrant so he can't talk about it. He can't go file a police report or go to the eyewitness news.

Dessalines - That's horrible

Louverture- Yes but, that's the reality of many immigrants without papers. Pedro was among one of the immigrants who were taken advantage of by some heartless Americans. Until one day he met a generous American who had a restaurant and needed someone to work days and nights. That first year Pedro worked and paid off everyone he owed. Once he and his family were free he started saving 95% of his income . He told me he only ate at the restaurant, so he didn't buy any food. Since Tia didn't have to cook for him his rent was less. He got a second job at my job and only slept 4 hours a day. Every time he saved up to ten thousand dollars, he would send it back home and his dad would buy land by the beach for him. After buying 10 different lands in different cities or neighborhoods, he started building on the lands one by one.

Dessalines - Ten different lands though? What do you mean by that?

Louverture- Pedro's dad went to 10 different popular cities or tourist areas and bought lands. He started building apartment complexes and stores to rent to foreigners, also known as immigrants, who moved to Mexico for a better life. He told me he was renting out a 2-bedroom apartment by the beach for two thousand dollars a month by the beach. Can you believe it? With the money from the apartments and from what he was making in the US, he started the second apartment complex that one was a luxury rental. You know he was making a lump sum of money out of each apartment. After that he built resorts. He even invested in his family farm, sold the crops at the restaurant and used it for the resort to feed the tourists.

Dessalines - Wait, his family had farms? So why didn't they farm and sell their crops instead of sacrificing themselves?

Louverture- I asked him the same thing. You would not believe what he told me.

Dessalines - What?

Louverture- number one was the drug trade, everyone in his town were forced to cultivate what the drug mafias told them too, so around the time he was a child they had abandoned their lands and moved to the slums of Mexico in order to not get involved. Number two, when things got better in their hometown they didn't have enough money to cultivate all those massive lands.

Dessalines- Wow I had no idea that the drug trade affected the Mexican lives too, especially farmers like Pedro family. We see lots of Mexicans in America but we don't know if they are fighting a war on drugs like the Americans are.

Louverture- Oh yes the American people have no clue and they are bitter about it; but the, American businessmen want Mexicans to come over so they can pay them cheap labor without any benefits. That is the only reason why they choose to hire illegal Aliens instead of Americans

Dessalines - Illegal Alien, I do not like that word at all, it sounds like the person is coming from out of space (rolled eyes) but if an illegal immigrant gets hurt on the job that's their problem; they can't do a thing about it. If anything, the immigrant will get deported right.

Louverture- That's right, thanks God Pedro was blessed. He was able to go back home in 6 years as a rich man. But there are so many immigrants who don't have the same ending as Pedro. Some are being blackmailed to get deported by their employer if they ask for better pay or even take a sick day. It's no joke, but thanks God Pedro was able to work hard, pay for the life of his family, and go back home as a king. I will show you his IG and you can see how this Mexican king is living it large now.

(Both scroll down Pedro's IG and look at his pictures.)

Dessalines - That's what's up! I'm happy for him. He is the true definition of: **Fuck the American Dream**! For real create your own path; live your own dream. I always hear about people who get killed on the border or get mistreated. But, it's my first time hearing about someone like Pedro. For some reason it's always the negative stories we know of as if God doesn't hear the immigrants' cry. Pedro's story should be shared with immigrants all over the world who come here. We all should know what Pedro did and we all can be able to do something similar in our own country for real.

Louverture- Yeah you're right, but I don't know about sleeping for only 4 hours and not having a social life. Evidently that's what worked for Pedro; each person has to see what works for them and make it happen.

Dessalines - You right. Everyone's journey is different and not everyone's path is the same. You see what happened to my Jamaican friend?

Louverture- who?

Dessalines- You remember Devan?

Louverture- Of course I remember Devan! What happened to Devan?

Dessalines -   He got deported for some absurdity.

Louverture – Are you serious? How? When did this shit happen? He was a nerd! He loves dance hall and smokes his weed that's about it

Dessalines - Yeah man messing with this girl named Becky and she got him in trouble.

Louverture- What, was she underage or something?

Dessalines - Not even. She was 20 and he was 19 at the time. So technically she was older than him.

Louverture- Wow, those cops probably needed to make their arrest for the month so Devan was their Prey.

Dessalines- What? What do you mean?

Louverture- You probably don't know but cops have to make curtain arrest for each month?

Dessalines- No I had no idea! And that doesn't even make sense for the system to be built like that. So, their job is not to protect but to arrest human beings so they can get paid.

Louverture- Technically yes, if not they will lose their job for not being vigilant.

Dessalines- Wow this is a capitalist country to the core. Now I truly understand why so many innocent black men are in prison.

Louverture- yup, it is sad but that's how the American system is built, that is their techniques to keep their prisons full and continue to make money off the prisoners. Cops are forced to go to certain neighborhoods so they can unlawfully make arrestations in order to make their little check. But Little did they know the system is using them too!

Dessalines- That's sickening for a human being to destroy another human being's life in exchange for a little paycheck and little do they know that comes with a generational curse to themselves and their loved ones. That's undignified, how did you know?

Louverture- I know for fact that's what happened to Abebe and Devan because it happened to me and many of my friends. I remember the last time I was arrested; after the cops threw me behind the back of his car he said to his partner, he can relax now he made his final arrest for the month. That's when I understood the pyramids scam and it dawned on me that the system was scamming me, using me so that the American economy can flow. That reality pushes me to change and gives me the urge to not want to be part of the American society anymore.

Dessalines- I definitely understand why you don't want to live in America anymore. I didn't even have those hatred experiences and I don't want to be part of this society; I see too many innocent lives vanish like leaves falling from a tree branch in the fall. Now I just want to live in a country where people are flourishing like the trees in spring.

Louverture- Me too, but to tell you the truth I don't have a problem with this country I just have a problem with the system that was inspired by Jim Crow and Willie Lynch. I can't live and invest in a country that I know the system was built to enslave people like me in all aspects of life. I just can't anymore, I want to live how Devan is living, and I am working toward that goal as we speak..

Dessalines- Oh yes I totally agree with you. Devan is really living the ideal life right now. You see what the enemy meant for evil God used it to build Devan up and put him in a higher state.

Louverture- Yes God did! God is in every situation for fact. But who was the girl Devan was hanging out with? Is she one of the girls from your school?

Dessalines- No! She is this white girl who moved from the suburb to Brooklyn he used to date.

Louverture- How? He always talked about how black women are empresses and that he will never date a white woman and he was dating one of them. That's this same hypocrisy that will embrace you in the long run.

Dessalines - Yes, and it definitely embarrassed Devan. But Devan was young and loved to have a good time and the girl was his neighbor who wanted to explore the Brooklyn culture and also love to have a good time. They both smoked weed and enjoyed each other's company. Until that day he was at the park by his house smoking a joint with her; next thing you know police pulled up and took both of them to the precinct. Maliciously Becky said he was trying to sell her some weed and that's the first time she met him. Devan told the truth, but you know they didn't believe him. They sent him straight to the county. The judge gave him probation and after his trial they took him to ICE. Couple months after he was in Jamaica.

Louverture- what do you mean? Just like that? He didn't have a lawyer?

Dessalines - Well you know some public defender, but we know how that goes. The police didn't even take Becky's name down when he went to the precinct. She was free, she went on living her life. I can't believe how Devan always talks about those types of situations and he ends up attracting it. After his situation I realized it's really important to watch what I talk about for real, because you will attract it!

Louverture- That is extremely important especially if you put all your emotions into it. Remember in the movie "The Secret" they talk about that. I am shocked right now, this entire time I saw Devan on social media I thought he was working for some overseas organization and he made the decision to move out of America.

Dessalines - No that was not his case at all.

Louverture- So what happened to him when he got to Jamaica?

Dessalines - When he first got there he was sorrowful, down, and miserable. Devan was supposed to graduate college with me in May, but instead he was walking out of this country. Chained up like a slave they were sending back to his plantation.

Louverture- That's terrible! You know that was racial profiling and white privilege at its finest. Because Devan is Jamaican he has to be selling weed. Plus, Becky just happens to be innocent because she is white.

Dessalines - Yes that definitely was racial profiling, but you know Devan had no money, he is a black man and an immigrant at that. His mom is an immigrant who doesn't know the system, so he had no one to speak for him nor defend him. But look on the bright side, Devan received his college diplomas!

Louverture- Really, He worked hard for it too. How did that happen?

Dessalines - As we know, Devan was the life of the party so you know he was always submitting his papers extra early so he can have a great time when he went clubbing. So, we were planning on going to Virginia beach for a weekend then to some fraternity party at a couple of Black colleges and at the end we were going to head to Miami beach with a bunch of friends and party for 7 days nonstop. So, he submitted his finals on Blackboard literally a couple days before he got locked up.

Louverture- Really, that's God's plan right there! Only a road trip of partying would make Devan submit his finals early.

Dessalines- (laughs) he was literally planning on enjoying the end of his senior year without worrying about a thing, and Devan knew he was about to come back wasted. There's no way he would have recovered from all that parting and write some finals when he got back.

Louverture- God is in everything for real. God knows Devan, so he made things happen like that for his party animal self. You remember that time I came over in your dorm for homecoming weekend; Devan was singing in the dorm at 4 am coming from that basement party? I am a party animal, and I don't sleep at all (both laugh)

Dessalines - When he thought he was getting ready for a road trip of parting; God said no my son you are going back home! I got better plans for you!

(both laugh out loud)

Louverture-And that's what really happened for real. Devan wanted to live the American dream. Working a 9 to 5, living in the suburb with his family taking a 2-week vacation once a year type of life, but we know Devan wouldn't survive in that misery!

Dessalines- Wow the American Dream! I never thought of it like that. I wonder if it's that same misery that is causing some people to be miserable and addicted in the suburbs.

Louverture- You never know, but 2 weeks of vacation would not be enough for Devan for fact

Dessalines- Now he is living the island dream!

Louverture- I always see him posting on a mansion by the beach on acres of land with every fruit you can think of.

Dessalines- Oh yes now he lives with his island wife, works 10 to 2 and takes 3 months of vacation a year with a great salary. Plus, he has businesses in Montego Bay, Kingston, and Portmore!

Louverture- How did that happen? Rewind tell me what happened when he got to Jamaica and how did he get that successful in a poor country?

Dessalines- You know what he told me when I went to see him?

Louverture -Wait you went to see him?

Dessalines- Yes I went with his mom; you know I was supposed to go on that road trip with him. So, we also planned on being in class all week before the trip. When I didn't see him in class the first day I signed him in and texted him. After class I called him and his phone was turned off. I went to his dorm room and his roommate told me he is still at home in Brooklyn and he left Friday after his 2pm class. So, I checked back later he was still not back. The next day the same thing happened, so I called his house phone in BK. Then his mom told me what happened. I didn't tell anybody in school, you know how college kids can be very judgmental for no reason.

Louverture- tell me about it

Dessalines- I swear college kids are struggling, barely passing accounting, but walking around like they are the V.P at JP Morgan. So, I kept it to myself and continued to sign him in. I even went to Devan's other classes and signed him in. You know those professors only know you by number, so I did that with no worries. I called his mom every day to make sure she was okay, you know that's her only son too, that's her only child, her pride and joy.

Louverture- That must have been really hard for her!

Dessalines - Yeah it was. When she got the deportation news she called me screaming patois on the phone for 30 minutes straight. The only thing I understood out of the conversation was my baby deported, fucking Babylon! That was 2 days before we graduated college.

Louverture- You see what I mean, you see why us Black immigrants should take what we can get and get out of this country!

Dessalines - I know, I know, But you know what? That was all part of God's plans. After that phone call from his mom I went straight to Brooklyn to see her. I walked in their 1-bedroom apartment that smelled straight up like weed and curry. She offered me a spliff so we smoked and talked about what we can do when her son gets to Jamaica. He called her when I was there, and we spoke for a few. Devan was down, his energy was low, he sounded like he didn't even want to live anymore. So, I told Devan you are still breathing? You know the law of attraction so put what you have been learning and teaching me to the test. So, you can attract better and manifest all the positivity out of your situation. And remember God is with you! Those were the last words I said to him before he left America.

Louverture- That's true what you told him, when life gets thought, you really have to look at the good out of the hardship and believe that God will carry you through.

Dessalines- That is true, I am learning about that more now, since I see how your life and Devan's had transformed by only focusing on the good out of a horrific situation.

Louverture- I am glad you are!

Dessalines- Thank You; So, after graduation, Devan's mom told me she took some time off from work to go see Devan in Jamaica. I got him all his books that were in his dorm room, you know the self-help books and the quantum physics books he was reading plus his clothes that were in his dorm room and I gave them to his mom to take out there. Devan had a library of books on those subjects.

Louverture- I saw them the last time I was in your school, but you never read any of those books right.

Dessalines- You know I was busy working fulltime and going to school full time, After I was done with school I had to find a job. Then I had to work so I never really have the time to read any of those books you and Devan are always preaching me about. (rolled her eyes)

Louverture- I hope you make time to start reading now because you see that dream you were chasing can't even pay your student loan depths.

Dessalines- Trust me I will Start reading. I understand the system now and I no longer want to be a statistic. But let me finish telling you about Devan.

Louverture- Yes please continue, I want to know all the details

Dessalines- So, after Devan's mother came back, she told me how sad and down he was. Devan was not even parting; he was not going to the beach or anything; he just stayed home depressed about the pass he could not change. So, I called him on WhatsApp. We spoke about life and what was happening in this country. I even told him how I signed him up in class every day. I even told him, he also needs to practice what he preaches and start reading all of those books he used to read in his dorm room because he was always positive and only saw positive out of any situation. So, a couple weeks later he called me and told me how his mom received his diplomas in the mail. I could hear the sense of relief in his voice. He also told me after he spoke to me he started praying again and doing positive affirmations. That positive affirmation definitely brought his spirit up. He called me on a video call a month later with a suit on, telling me how he got a job in the Jamaican government. His diplomas surely helped him. Since his mom had opened a small business out there for him, he took his first paycheck and invested all of it in the business knowing that his business would only expand. Now he was working close to the president of Jamaica, he couldn't run the business anymore. He made his mom quit her home health aide job and her cleaning jobs to come run the business.

Louverture- That's a blessing for real, Devan would never get a job like that if he was still in America. Plus, his mother will not be able to quit her job before she turns 65 if Devan was in America.

Dessalines- there is always a positive out of a negative situation for real. So, Devan's mother collected all her money and moved to Jamaica in 9 months with One hundred thousand dollars. She cashed out her 401k and all her other savings. She went to her country real humble with lots of money in her carry-on bag. That's when I went to Jamaica with her. I didn't know she had that much money with her, but I suspected her because she even went to the bathroom with that carry-on bag (laughs). We flew first class and when we landed we were treated like celebrities. Her house was built and furnished. It took her 15 years to build that house while she was living in a tiny one-bedroom apartment in Brooklyn with her son. Devan welcomed me with ice-cold red stripes and fresh weed from their backyard.

Louverture- That's beautiful, I am so happy for him and his mom. They deserve it.

Dessalines- Yes, You should see how they are living now, compared to how they were living in Brooklyn. Devan made me see the life I can be living in my own country, how my degree has more value in third-world countries than in America. Devan was driving nice cars, making lots of money while living in his mom's mansion, her retired home. When I was there we partied every night and Devan went to work every day, just like we did in college. We were in our 20's so what did you expect us to do? But he was very smart with his money; he showed me a property he bought by the beach and the mansion he wanted to build in it. Devan had drivers, maids, chefs. He was living the dream!

Louverture- Really, I hope Devan was not involved in any corruption working in the government.

Dessalines - Never! He knows better to get involve in that

Louverture-We both know of all the corruption that takes place in Many countries that's why I mention it. I really hope he keeps his hands clean and his heart pure.

Dessalines- I definitely see what you mean corruption is one of the main reasons some countries cannot get out of poverty for fact. But Devan believed in karma, especially after he found out what happened to Becky, the girl that lied about him. He told me that Becky was in jail with a drug dealer record.

Louverture- You see now that's her karma! If she didn't lie on him, he probably would have been able to travel back to the US without a problem. Now look what ended up happening to her conniving self. She wanted to screw Devan's life over, playing the innocent game, but look what she ended up doing to herself. That's why you have to be careful of what you say or do in this life.

Dessalines- That's true, because you will reap what you sow. But Devan is marvelous, he said America is not heaven. He was here for many years before, plus he got what he wanted from America already. There is no need for him to want to come back.

Louverture- Yes. Plus, he doesn't have to worry about student loans anyways. He have that good karma on his side

Dessalines- For real! He knows what goes around does come back around so he does all his affairs right. You know his mom has resorts and apartments in Jamaica now, and plus he is the only child so they invest most of their profits.

Louverture- That's great, But you know what I want to know what he does in the government?

Dessalines- He works with the minister of education; Devan was one of the experts who wanted to change Jamaica's school system. Because of him, Marcus Garvey's books and biography is mandatory in all Jamaica's school systems along with many other books that focus on Black history, especially Black history before slavery, and books that's empowering the mind.

Louverture- Wow that's what's up! That's definitely God's plan that he had gotten deported. What was his major in school again?

Dessalines- He was a double major in Political Science and Sociology, and a minor in African Studies.

Louverture- America missed out on an intelligent man who could have made America a better society!

Dessalines- But you know what, America doesn't need Devan. He is a Black man with a thick accent and you and I know exactly where they want his immigrant self, driving a taxi or on that factory line. But now Devan got his mansion by the beach, driving a Benz, he has a beautiful Jamaican wife that's just like him, 2 book nerds who know how to enjoy life. (both laugh). He is making his country great living his best life.

Louverture- that's a beautiful story, I want to be like Devan right now, all I need is my beautiful Haitian wife by my side.

Dessalines- (rolled her eyes) Yea okay. Anyways his mom got married too; she married this big billionaire from England, technically he is a Jamaican Diaspora who lived in England for many years

Louverture- Oh really, They are both in Jamaica living their best lives.

Dessalines- They surely are. Her house is an Airbnb that's making money on a regular while she travels and lives her best life in her late 40s with her husband. Her businesses are growing, she's creating jobs, providing her people with better and quality lifestyles. What happened to Devan and his mom made me realize, when life is not going as planned be grateful, because God's plan is always the best plan!

Louverture- Amen to that! Let me know the next time you are flying to Jamaica and I'll definitely come with you. We can stay in Devan mother's Airbnb.

Dessalines- I'll definitely do that. Every time I Think about Devan, all the great things he has accomplished in his country makes me want to move back home.

Louverture- Yeah I would too if I was you, I am working on that as you know. But what are you doing for yourself? What are your plans to get yourself out of America? So, we can live this Island dream together.

Dessalines- I don't know yet.

Louverture- You will know soon; you already have the recipe for the pie.

Dessalines- What do you mean I have the recipe for the pie? What pie has to do with me planning on leaving America.

Louverture- We both have the recipe to the pie. But, not every immigrant or American grasps it.

Dessalines- What recipe to what pie? You are always using some terminology you made up. Be direct, tell me about this pie.

Louverture- Oh, you really don't know.

Dessalines- No I do not know, I don't even like pie anyways

Louverture- Alright, You don't like pies? Then how did you get the recipe to the pie if you don't like pie?

Dessalines - Really? What are you talking about? Stop playing games!

Louverture- (laugh) okay, You never heard of the expression I got a piece of the pie?

Dessalines - (bate her eyes) Yeah! But where are you going with this?

Louverture- What is that piece of the pie?

Dessalines- I am not going to answer you, you play too much.

Louverture- You know you love when I play with you like that.

Dessalines- whatever (give him a serious stare)

Louverture- Sorry serious lady. But what is that piece of a pie? Isn't it a home in the suburb, a 2- family car and 2 .5 healthy kids, with a job that has benefits? You know, what they call the American dream

Dessalines - Yes I know. So, what is the recipe of the pie? It should be more than a home in the suburb, and a job behind a desk in a little cubical right.

Louverture - Yes the recipe of the pie is way more than what the American dream has to offer to us. It's a leadership mentality, forever improving, always wanting more, never too comfortable and always grateful.

Dessalines Oh ok, people like Trump, Carnegie, and Shawn Carter (Jay-Z). They have the recipe for that pie.

Louverture- (laughs) You have to talk about Trump. His name has to roll out your tongue right. I wouldn't be surprised if you voted for him.

Dessalines - I'm stating facts, and you know I'm right. We might not like his way of doing politics and many other things about him, but remember no one is perfect but God. I believe everyone has a lesson to teach us, but if we are only focusing on their weakness it will blind us and we will not grasp their lesson. I know you secretly like how he built his empires, I remember when you used to read all the books he read that had helped him build his empire. And to answer your question about voting, I have a green card so I don't have the right to vote.

Louverture - that's right I forgot you didn't change your nationality. But you right, Jay- Z and Kanye West are great examples for anyone to follow.

Dessalines-. But you know what Black American leaders like Jay-Z are paving the path for Black Americans nationwide. Us immigrants, we see, we understand, we admire the Leaders in American!

Louverture - Since slavery they have being fighting for each other, stand up for each other. Creating opportunities for one another. They are showing us immigrants how to live in our own country. How we should create jobs and help out each other in time of need. Remember how it was always a fight between Black Americans and us black immigrants when we were in high school? They felt like they had to protect each other and their communities. Since society thought them we were different from each other and created a conflict between us. But little by little we realize that we are all one race, one skin color and we face the same obstacles.

Dessalines - That is true I admire my Black American Brothers and sisters for their unity, strength and love for one another. If they knew better when we were kids they would have treated us better.

Louverture- That's a fact! I remember when we were kids we fought a lot like many siblings do. But now we understand we are one, and it's all love and respect and of course we are about our businesses and building each other up.

Dessalines -- Yes, now it is our time to be bosses and create jobs for millions in the neighborhoods that gave us thick skins.

Louverture- But, we will always be immigrants who came for a piece of the American pie to the Law and some Americans. Now America is no longer sharing. Entrepreneurs like myself, we have the recipe to make our own pie, so we are taking the recipe and making our pie where we are loved and appreciated.

Dessalines - I understand, things have changed a lot for us immigrants in this country, and we are better off in our own territory. But Black Americans are out here conquering this whole country plus many other countries. They are the leaders of the Black movement and I respect them for that,

Louverture- Black immigrants are part of this movement too, but Black Americans have been preaching positivity, love and unity since the 1950's. Martin Luther King only preached love and unity so it is only right that many years later his message continues to influence the Black Americans. The Black Americans are the world leaders and influencers for real, but I don't even think they know it yet.

Dessalines- Some do and the ones who don't will know soon.

Louverture- Yes they will. Just like us Haitians we didn't know we were the leaders for many blacks who were enslaved in plantations all over the world until after we revolted. Right after that every Haitian knew their strength and the fact that they were the leaders of the blacks worldwide The Haitians made it their personal business to free as many enslaved blacks they could off.

Dessalines- We called our creator the God of all gods. That's how we won the Battle of Vertieres in November 18, 1803 and became the first black republic on January 1st, 1804.

Louverture- Some people want to discredit us and say that we did voodoo. But me I say, we believed that we could've liberated ourselves from slavery, we called on the God of the most high for help and we did the unthinkable man and women stood tall and defeated the number one army at the time.

Dessalines - Yes black men and women fought side by side for 12 hours nonstop and won the victory. If some people want to choose to live by ignorance because they don't want to believe God freed the Haitians and helped them win the war against France, then that's on them. But us, we know the truth and we will live by the truth and teach our children the truth. We might have some political differences in Haiti but we are one country. But America is divided into two republics sharing 1 land, one flag. They need to solve that problem before they go to people's countries telling them how to live. But who will stand up and tell Americans how to live? What is right or what is wrong?

Louverture- Their children, their children will learn about their wicked ways and judge them in the world court of law. But what I admire about Black Americans is that they know how to build, how to properly protest and create positive change in their community and system.

Dessalines- Yes that's true, us Black immigrants can learn a lot from them and start implementing those great qualities in our own lands. It is time for us to stop pointing fingers and start forgiving one another as a human race. I Know I can be guilty of that and I am learning to change that about myself. Our creator forgives us daily without remembering our wrongdoing. We are made in our creator's image, so we have the capability to forgive, love and live in peace!

Louverture- Yes love, that's why I love. You are pure love, and you always see God's love in every situation. But the ones with innocent bloods in their hands will pay for their wrong doings.

Dessalines- that is true Karma is real, the ones who did good will reap goodness and the ones who did wrong will reap their wrong doings as well. That is just the law of nature. God doesn't punish mankind; mankind punishes themselves by their wrong doings and blames God for it instead of owning up to it and changing their ways of living.

Louverture- Yes, yes. That's why I love talking to you, Only some with a pure heart can admit to those words that just came out of your mouth.

Dessalines- Only a real person like yourself will agree with me without being argumentative. To tell you the truth I find it important for us to continue what our ancestors started in Latin America. They freed all those Spanish countries from their masters with their resources. They even freed American slaves too. I bet the Americans didn't know they were the first boat people who made the voyage on a banana boat.

Louverture- Yes. Haitians had the policy. Any runaway slave was welcome to Haiti, and we gave them food, land, and clothing. That's something else we did with our resources. I'm proud to say that, and true historians know that is a fact. That's one of the many reasons why white countries didn't want to do business with us; they knew their slaves were coming to Haiti by the hundreds. So, they put the embargo on us so we couldn't continue freeing our brothers and sisters. And guess what we did? We continued to take them in and use our resources to make sure they were good, while we were paying

France back for gaining our freedom. We had to pay For our freedom while the Collins who committed many crimes got to live freely.

Dessalines - That's preposterous that us human beings had to pay our oppressors, we had to pay France because we believe in liberty for all human race, we had to pay because we believed slavery was wrong, and the way white people treated the black race was immoral. What they did to us they would never even dare to mistreat their dog in that matter, an animal at that.

Louverture- It's okay, we can only fight hate with divine love just like Nelson Mandela. The love we send will come back to us and our children, the hate they send will definitely go back to them and their children. That is the law of nature, energy you put out is guaranteed to come back to you.

Dessalines - That is true, after all you know better you must do better. If any children of the French, colonizers were not like their fathers, they would return the money their ancestors forced the Haitians to pay them. If they did, They would have a heart of love and understanding to say no, our forefathers were ignorant and heartless individuals who chased nothing but greed. We are sorry and this is your money. We are sorry for taking it in the past and we are giving you all of your billions of dollars back. We are sorry for the pain and humiliation we caused you for generations.

Louverture- That's on them if they choose to, but I know I rely on myself and my creator so I know my country will prosper no matter what! But if you want to take it there make sure to include all the countries who colonized and enslaved us blacks and demanded the golds that are display in their cathedrals, the diamonds that are crowning their queen and princesses heads, the monuments in their museums, plus the animals who are in their zoos who need to live in the wild in Africa like God intended. We cannot only speak for ourselves we have to speak for the blacks worldwide!

Dessalines- you are right, and if any children of the Haitian liberators were like their forefathers, they would've stood in the world court of law and demanded that France give the Haitians their money back. Just like the Black Americans are standing up and asking for their 40 acres and their mulls that the American government owes them. Imagine if every country in the world who were exploited in the name of slavery did that. Just imagine if every country stood up tall in front of their oppressors, the white supremacy and demanded everything that was taken from them.

Louverture- I can see it very clearly in my vision. The world will definitely be a better place. It is time that we take full control of our lives, our resources and our lands period!

Dessalines - Really, you sound like you are ready to go to war.

Louverture- Oh, of course not. We are smarter human beings. I am ready to use my intellect and say justice must be done. We shall get what is ours as a people, it is only fair. Don't get me wrong, I'm all about peace and love. We are all one human race and we should focus on the bigger picture and unite with our creator but the oppressors can't seem to comprehend that. Justice shall be done, as we both know justice is not given but taken!

Dessalines - You right, justice with peace will be done! But leave it to God.

Louverture- It is in God's hands he is with us every step of the way. We are taking actions so the words can get across and for everyone on the face of the earth to know that we are revolting.

Dessalines - What we should do as a people? So, you want us to put all our energy on showing Black people how intelligent and powerful we are?

Louverture- I think we know that already. Plus, it is obvious that we also know when we unite we can conquer all things.

Dessalines - For fact! you also want Black Americans to know that they are the influencers, they are raising Black vibrations all over the world with their self-love movement.

Louverture- They know, but us the people who have been oppressed by a corrupted system, we need to work on ourselves individually so we can make a collective change.

Dessalines- I definitely agree we have to be fulfilled in order to make an effective change.

Louverture- You my darling, how are you fulfilling yourself in order to be part of the global change.

Dessalines- (looks at her watch) really number 1 please stop calling me your darling, number 2 you're really asking me what I am about to do when all you do is talk without walking. I am going home to start dinner before my mom gets back from work. I will talk to you later.

Louverture - Really you're mad, and that's how you view me? You think I am all talk? Don't worry, I will show you from now on. I am working on a lot of big things. You will soon see what I am capable of.

Dessalines - I am not mad, but walk your talk as I go cook my creole dish

Louverture- Okay love, you will see. I have to go to my meeting soon. But I am looking forward to tasting your griyo one day

Dessalines- You're always going to some meeting, what's that about?

Louverture- When the time's right I'll take you with me.

Dessalines- I don't know about that but you better be careful

Louverture- trust me you will love it.

Dessalines- Only God knows (waves as she walks away) bye see you later, have fun at your meeting

As she walks inside her home Louverture admires the way her waist moves like a folkloric dancer. He starts to think how one day he will ask his longtime friend to be his wife. Because life with her is worth living. He walks away with hope in his heart, while he thinks of ways to show his love to his best friend.

Weeks went by and the two friends have not heard from each other. They were both busy, working on themselves, making money and investing in their personal dreams while they were

investing in themselves. One Friday afternoon
Toussaint reaches out to Dessalines

Scene 2

Louverture - (sits in his car as he phones Dessalines) Hello

Dessalines - Hey stranger, sak passe?

Louverture - How's everything?

Dessalines - I am great, I was just thinking about you today when I was leaving work.

Louverture- (smiling) Oh really, what an honor to be in your precious mind. I am outside your house, come tell me all about it. I am all ears my darling.

Dessalines- What do you mean you are outside my house? What did I tell you about that? What if my boyfriend was here?

Louverture- Then you will tell your boyfriend your real man is outside, and he has to go.

Dessalines - Is that so? You better be quiet before I don't come outside anymore.

Louverture- I am sorry you know I was playing with you.

Dessalines - Yea okay, Give me 5 mins. I'm coming

As Dessalines walks out her house everyone who was outside stops to admire how the sun is shining on her dark chocolate skin, as her jet-black kinky hair bounces on her collarbones. Dessalines is about 5-5 and weighs 130 pounds with dark brown eyes and high cheekbones. Her teeth are whiter

than pearls and she is shaped like the number 8.
She looks like a Nubian queen, a beauty like hers
was hard not to stare. She waves at Louverture so
he can come sit on her front steps.

Louverture - (as he walks out of the car) hey love. I would love to know why I was on your mind all day

Dessalines - Relax, it was only this afternoon. And it is not that serious. Some of my colleagues started a conversation which turned into a debate and almost into an argument

Louverture - What was it about?

Dessalines- Culture gentrification!

Louverture- That's a sensitive conversation to have, especially with the ones who feel and are really oppressed by it. What did you say?

Dessalines- Me? I don't get involved in those conversations anymore. Especially with people who are close minded and not willing to understand your point of view.

Louverture- Yes that conversation can drain someone's energy and put them in a low vibration. And once someone is at a low vibration, they can't really accomplish anything from a low state of mind.

Dessalines- I learned my lesson, that is why I sat quietly and ate my lunch at peace.

Louverture-So what happened? I know how you love to voice your opinion

Dessalines- Let me tell you how Lakiesha, you know the conscious sister at my job, she got mad at me a couple years ago when I was explaining to her how she should be happy to see Black American culture exposed everywhere. How it was the same thing for Greece one time. She screamed and said it is not the same, I am an immigrant I will never get it. So, I said you are probably right so explain it to me. Then she explains that Black Americans call it cultural appropriation because other races, especially whites will ridicule how we dress, wear our hair and anything you can think about. Then go on to copy all of our culture and have the nerves to pretend they invented it.

Louverture- That is true, she is right about that, when it is us doing it they call it ghetto but once it is them doing it they call it the latest fashion.

Dessalines- I agreed with her too, then I told her 10 years from now Black Americans will conquer the entire world just like Greece did. You know how The Romans went to conquer Greece, but in the end Greece ended up conquering Rome and the whole world by influencing everyone with their culture.

Louverture- What did Lakisha say?

Dessalines - She didn't get it. She said the Roman and the Greece were both white. Then I told her, slavery didn't start in Africa; White people were enslaving each other for centuries before they got their hands on the African slave ships. And Not everything is black and white in this world so if we change the way we look at a situation the situation must change.

Louverture - Yeah I see what you mean, and I agree with you 100% but you have to understand they come from a generation of trauma. Plus, they were thought to hate themselves. It needs deep meditation and praying, reading, and sometime therapy to get over generational trauma

Dessalines- I agree but remember Black immigrants went through the same hardships and despair from slavery. We were mistreated in our own lands

Louverture- Yes but we didn't face oppression or police brutality in a white privilege society until we came to America. Do you know the history of policing in the United States of America?

Dessalines- No

Louverture- Doing slavery there where slave catchers, and after slavery ended those slave catchers didn't have a job so the policing was created so they can continue the arras Black Americans.

Dessalines- are you serious, I had no idea

Louverture- That's another topic for another day, but you're right. All Blacks were going through it but the American system has their foot on Black American neck trying to stop them from elevating. But now, it is a new era and we are evolving in all aspects of life. At the end of the day Blacks are conquering the world just like the Greeks did with their literature, math, sciences, medicines, the arts, sports, spirituality and many more.

Dessalines- Somebody needs to tell Sean Combs that, because he posted something on Instagram regarding that and that's how the conversation started at work. Wait I am going to read it for you (picks up phone scrolled down and starts reading the post). "Our culture is a global resource, let's not play ourselves and wake up one day and not own our own culture. Tighten up on your contracts, tighten up on your deals. Demand OWNERSHIP! Demand EQUITY! Protect your culture. IT'S FOR EVERYONE TO ENJOY BUT FOR US TO OWN!" You hear that, wait (stops and pauses to re-read the post to herself) he is saying the same thing we are saying. Ownership is how the Greeks were able to preserve their culture while they influenced the whole world.

Louverture - Sean Combs is right. It is not 1920 nor the 1800s, the world has changed. This whole world we knew of has changed, and we need to understand that. Everyone who is creating should take Sean's advice and own their masterpieces so the rest of the world can enjoy for many generations to come and to study and analyze blacks creativities in universities. What were your colleagues' arguments about the comment Sean posted?

Dessalines- It is not even worth mentioning (rolls her eyes) They believe no one should enjoy what Black Americans create but Black Americans. They even went to say no Black immigrants shouldn't celebrate Black History Month because it is only about Black Americans' accomplishments. They don't even understand how much the Black diaspora helped Black Americans. It sounds like they wanted to segregate themselves from the rest of the world. They misinterpreted Diddy's message for fact!

Louverture- People like that are best to ignore and carry on. Sean Combs also known as Puff Daddy is a legend, an icon, we need to respect him and the contribution he made to the American society. He is teaching us Blacks the importance of having all rights to all that we produce and create just like the great thinker Plato. We know Plato's masterpiece and we respect Greece for all their great thinkers. The post was just preparation for the new era we are now in. We are now living in a time where every man will literally reap what they sow. Everyone will get to enjoy the fruit of their labor. Mankind is intelligent; we know how to maneuver, and we are helping one another in the process. That was his intention behind the post. But there are people like you and your colleagues who create their own conclusion

Dessalines - (laughs) Really? You know I believe Black inventors are wiser now. Life is not how it used to be and we are adapting to this new lifestyle rapidly.

Louverture - You know I love to tease you, but what you said is true we are wiser and positive changes are here for us all. So, let's enjoy life while we are creating generational wealth. I truly admire Sean Combs' works and the way he does business, that's why I am working on becoming who God has created me to be for when he comes looking for me I will be prepared!

Dessalines - Okay! Let me know when you are going to meet Mr. Comb, I will definitely come with you. But what I was trying to say before is this; Lakisha needs to understand that history does repeat itself. Harriet Tubman had to identify herself with Moses in order to free many slaves from the south, just like Moses freed the Israelites. She didn't look at the differences, but only focused on the fact that they are both God's child. What God did for Moses he could do it for her too, and God did! We need to get our minds out of that brainwashed history class in high school that separates us from the rest of the world and be able to identify ourselves with everyone in the world in order to understand we are one human race.

Louverture - Yes, You hit it on the nail.

Dessalines- I can also feel that it is a new ERA; things are changing for the best. What Diddy wrote is an eye opener so people can value their artwork and take ownership. Black Americans should be happy to see how they are influencing the world. Us Black people from all over the globe, we are the blueprint! We are here with our full essence! Plus, we are here to stay! We are owning our works! We are securing our bags! We are traveling and living our best life while creating generational wealth!

Louverture- Wait, you're Black American now? You're an immigrant, you better chill. You heard what your President has been talking about. Now you are talking about "we." Since when you had an American passport.

Dessalines- What do you mean? I am an American, I am from the continent of North America so that makes me an American.

Louverture- Geographically speaking you are right. Someone from France, England, or Spain are considered Europeans. So, for example someone from Haiti, Mexico or Jamaica are considered Americans too because we are from the continent of the Americas.

Dessalines- Oh yes, we are all Americans. Plus, you know who's my president

Louverture- Yes Queen, that is why it is important to be knowledgeable and be able to share what you know. But I stop by to talk to you about something.

Dessalines- what is it? Everything okay?

Louverture- Yes everything is fine; I came here to talk to you about money. I feel like it is important to reach out to everyone I love and talk to them about what I know. The businesses that I started are evolving and I am even building my mansion by the beach in Haiti. Now I have made it, I have proof that what I have been doing works so I wanted to share it with you first. Since you know you were always there for me, and you know how much I love you

Dessalines- Yes like a sister

Louverture- what?

Dessalines- You love me like your sister and you are the brother I never had. But continue. I am proud of you, now I see you were not just talking, you actually were walking and talking. (give Louverture a hug)

Louverture- (hug Dessalines tight) Thank you, You have been there for me longer than anyone else I have ever known. I don't want to give you money because I know you will not take it from me so I want to tell you what I did, how I did it.

Dessalines- the old me yes but the new me will take both the money and the advice! (both laugh)

Louverture-Since I last saw you I left with this drive. The conversation we had gave me this ambition to do more than I was doing. I was inspired and motivated; So, I went within, I meditated and prayed asking God to direct my path. Next thing you know ideas started coming to me, ideas from the divine that helped me grow my businesses and the right business partners came knocking at my doorsteps. That is when I realize the importance of going within and to thoroughly know oneself and work on myself.

Dessalines- I am glad our conversation sparked a revolution within you, because it also did for me as well.

Louverture- I am happy to hear that; So, start to know the inner being who lives in this wonderful body and start working on you so you can vibrate higher, manifest, and create. If you are on a low vibration you will never see the bigger picture. Allow yourself to fail, allow others to fail too.

Dessalines- Just like God loves us even though we sin. Life is a marathon that we each will have to know how to run individually.

Louverture- But the race starts within!

Dessalines- You right. I have to get my mind right. I have to start seeing the positivity in everything, then we will be able to understand what life is really about. I see what you mean, the minute we start worrying about negativity that is happening, next thing you know we start attracting that lifestyle. I remember when I used to only focus on the injustices that are happening in the world. After a while it became my reality, my world, my experiences.

Louverture- Oh yes, I was there too. But now I am done, I can only focus on what is right, pure, and lovely. So, let's talk about how people are making money so I can attract more of that liberated lifestyle. Let's remain on a high vibration for real.

Dessalines - I feel better already just by thinking about how Tyler Perry owns his own production studio, a self-made black man. That is extraordinary. I only need to focus on all the goodness that is happening in front of my eyes

Louverture - Now you see what I have been talking about. If I worry about telling people to open their eyes and they are conquering the world, I will be going against the grain. I need to live my truth and they will understand it's our time! Like Lory Mentor said in her poem, "It's our time!" If I did go around screaming "It's our time," what do you think my Black American family will say to my immigrant self?

Dessalines - If you are at a protest they will definitely agree with you and start protesting with you.

Louverture- Yea but what If I was in your job or an institution and start screaming," It's our time".

Dessalines- People will definitely think you are crazy; I mean who does that

(Both laugh)

Louverture- That's why I will go to a protest and voice my opinion, but after that I will focus on my businesses, making my money and praying for them, for us while I elevate into my higher self and transfer my positive energy to everyone I meet. I need money to truly stand behind what I believe in right!

Dessalines - I totally agree with you, You are so right plus praying for someone is ten times better than preaching to an empty church

Louverture - Exactly, and it is easier too

Dessalines - The advantage of praying for others is that you are praying for yourself as well. In all spiritual books it says to pray for others, including your enemies. There is great power in prayer. I love this new era spiritualism because we don't have to fight physically anymore, we can just let our spirit guide us.

Louverture- Yes! I clearly see what you mean. So that's why everyone is so focused on mental health and how the mind operates, our spiritual self and being woke!

Dessalines - They are all connected. Us as a human race we are finally focusing on the inner self, the non-physical in general. We as a people are now understanding the importance of our health mentally and emotionally. That's why everyone in the world is standing up against this evil system called racism, built by white men with greed in their hearts and innocent blood in their hands.

Louverture- Yes, the entire world has woken up and we are freeing our souls from this 400 years of bondage.

Dessalines- we definitely are. Since the last time we spoke I have been doing some inner work myself. I started praying more and reading my bible, I even downloaded the bible app on my phone and I would read a biblical passage at work and pray silently during my lunch break. So, one time I wrote a biblical passage on my social media and a friend of mine commented, How can I be pro- black and a Christian. How can I worship the master's God who had enslaved us. So, I wrote back lest not forget where Christianity came from and how everyone in the bible is African. Remember Israel is in Africa, Egypt is in Africa, Queen Sheba who traveled to Jerusalem to experience the wisdom of King Solomon was from Ethiopia, and Ethiopia is in Africa. Jesus who died on the cross, resuscitated, and appeared to thousands preaching the message of love, the power of the mind was an African!

Louverture- You are so right, if you look at a map the truth is right in front of our face but we are blind to it because they didn't teach us Geography. Now it is time for us to teach ourselves. And take ownership.

Dessalines- To tell you the truth, Jesus the Christ came for all of us, but the Europeans became selfish with greed and took our spiritual book and made everything about skin color.

Louverture- Oh my goodness you are so right, The bible is our spiritual book. But the Europeans stole it and tried to Europeanize the bible so they can feel powerful. While they made us believe we were only worshiping the sun and moon, it is a form of control to make us believe we are illiterate. I mean how can we worship what our creator has created to serve us, when we can worship our creator, the God of all gods

Dessalines- exactly. that's why slavery lasted so long, they took our spiritual books, killed our leaders. Then they enslave us, physically, mentally and spiritually. The Haitians freed us physically by boldly revolting in 1804. But now after 400 years we are revolting and freeing ourselves mentally and spiritually. The 400 years is up!

Louverture- What do you mean the 400 years is up?

Dessalines- (pick up her phone scrolling) hold on let me read something to you then after that you will definitely understand. I landed on this passage one night. I was crying, praying to God and asking God, when will all this white supremacy brainwash be over? When will he free us from our oppressors?

Louverture- Ok I am listening.

Dessalines- It is in Genesis 15 verse 13 and 14 state, "God said to Abram, Your descendants will live in a land that is not their own, where they will be slaves and be oppressed for 400 years. But I will punish the nation they serve and after that they will come out with great wealth." Slavery started in 1619 and 2019 makes it exactly 400 years; I don't know about you but I believe in my covenant with God.

Louverture- You are so right; this is writing black on white but we as a people only focus on the obey your master crap they taught us. You are so intelligent and in tune. If you don't go within and do your own research you will truly be misguided. I am so thankful I stopped by today, I thought I was coming to teach you something and you ended up schooling me.

Dessalines- We are teaching each other; I share what I know with you and you do the same in return. So now you can continue telling me about the law of the mind so I can govern me.

Louverture- Okay, this is the best way I can explain it, We are all able to listen to our spirit that is allowing us to feel negative when we are talking, or thinking of a low vibration subject that does not make us feel good. And once we don't feel good mentally, more negative thoughts start popping in our heads and next thing you know we are on a low frequency and we can't even see clearly to manifest what we want. Our inner self, the spirit within us, is always communicating with us through our feelings and emotions.

Dessalines - I never heard some spiritual insight like this in church, and you know I have been in church all my life. I have been talking about spiritualism for years and now it's like I don't know a thing. I am re-analyzing everything now, questioning all truths. I believe knowing the science of the mind will definitely make life easier for me.

Louverture- You know most of the author's books I read quote passages in the bible.

Dessalines- Really, I am definitely going to start reading those books.

Louverture- You should, life's meant to be easy and joyful. That's why our spirit is trying to guide us to think and talk positively so we can do what we came to do on this earth. We have to be in a high vibration to be able to connect with our creator and listen to our creator. Honestly speaking, God always came through for me even when I was in a low state. I was the one who didn't feel worthy of communicating with him, but then I didn't know better. I didn't do better. Now I know, my creator and I are best friends.

Dessalines - I see what you mean. Some religions will have you feel stuck and make you feel like you are the worst being God ever created. Biblically speaking that is a lie, historically speaking that was all part of white supremacy plans so they could have better controlled non-whites. But now we know, God created us all in his image therefore we are perfect! I am now working on myself, letting go of all the negative brainwashing and beliefs about myself and about God. From now on I believe with all my heart that God loves me and cares for me no matter what!

Louverture- You have to in order to live a better life. Our creator is a loving and caring God, he created everything on earth for us human beings to enjoy. Self-image is truly important, because if we are feeling unworthy, trust me we will start looking like it, walking like it and acting like it too. I've been there so I know from experience of negative self-image and positive self-image about myself.

Dessalines- That's true

Louverture- Most people you see living large and happy are on a high vibration, that's why they are able to let their spirit guide them so they can accomplish what they came to earth for. Oprah did it, she's a living example.

Dessalines - She is a walking blueprint for fact

Louverture- can you believe Oprah was making 22 thousand a year in the 80's and she was able to multiply that to create billions. She was able to use her God given talent to make twenty-two thousand a year. She trusted God, she was thankful, and God gave her 10 times more. She took that lump sum of money, invested in herself, and opened businesses one by one giving people jobs and starting nonprofits to help others too.

Dessalines- That's a true queen, someone who came from nothing and allowed her creator to use her to become someone important. Actually, I want to be like Oprah, she did her thing with style and grace. She is indubitably inspirational. I will make sure to tell her that when I sit and have a conversation with her too.

Louverture- Once you go meet her I'll definitely come with you. You see how our energy just shifts just because we started talking about Oprah's success.

Dessalines - You are right! I can feel it, I am happy and excited for no reason. I mean once we started talking about Oprah and how she made her billions I just got immensely excited, and I just feel overly happy. I feel like I am the one who has billions of dollars in my bank account.

Louverture- That's the power of the mind, that's your spirit, your soul that's allowing you to feel terrific; telling you to keep going, listen to more things that's making you feel good. Engage in conversations that are making you feel at your best. Like they say, you know the truth once you hear the truth. It is your soul that is eternal, that is guiding you deep inside to the truth that God has engraved in your heart, in mankind's heart. It is important to listen to the voice inside and pay attention to the instructions of the creator. Plus, our soul is always guiding us on our path. But we have to understand the way that our soul communicates with us.

Dessalines - I Think I get it now, but if I'm wrong, correct me. So, by talking or thinking about something negative, your soul tells you that you are not on the right path of your true calling by making you feel bad. So that is a warning sign for you to stop!

Louverture - Yes, it is a warning for you to stop and start thinking happy thoughts. Whatever thoughts that will put a smile on your pretty face.

Dessalines - (rolls her eyes) Anyways! So, the minute you start thinking or talking positively you are happy, and you get excited about the simple things in life and that's your soul telling you that you are on the right path and stay there too right? And next thing you know ideas start penetrating your head, you are meeting the right people, you are at the right place at the right time, securing your money and making hundreds, thousands, millions and even billions of dollars. I love the sound of that.

Louverture - Yes me too. Now it is the time for everyone to start communicating through their souls to elevate and manifest themselves to their true state. There are young men and women who are making more than $20,000 a year. That's more than what Oprah was making when she just started.

Dessalines-There are others who are working in corporate or working in warehouses who are literally making $40,0000 a year some 2 times more. Imagine what they can do with that money.

Louverture- Yes a lot can be done with or without money, you just have to remain at a high frequency. It is all about the mind.

Dessalines - That is true, you are so right. That's how men and women are freeing themselves out of this prison system.

Louverture- That is true, while I was in prison, I took my time to work on myself, reading self-help books, thinking of different ways to make positive money, and living a more productive life. I know people who sit in the jail cells and think about the business they are going to do when they get home every single day and as soon as they come home, they get it done.

Dessalines- Oh yes, people in the hood are saying ex-inmates are coming home with superpowers. Like this young man I know in Jersey City. This young king came home in that same toxic environment he was selling drugs in and opened a sandwich deli. He is a superhero in my book. He realized that there are so many types of businesses he can do so he found the one that he loves. And I guess he loves subs.

Louverture- Plus his mind changed too, that's the first thing that took place. He saw himself differently and he acted differently. For example, a lion knows he is the king of the jungle so the lion moves like a king. I hope he opens a franchise out of his sandwich joint, that way he will be the supplier to many young men and women who are coming home from prison.

Dessalines- Yes that's a great idea, you always dream and think big.

Louverture- (blush) Thank you, coming from you it is an honor. But you know what I realize, every businessman is just like the drug dealer, or hustler. They are both risk takers, both are risking their money while the drug dealers are also risking their freedom and their own life. When both types of businesses end up doing great each type of businessman will reap what they sow. The man who is selling products to add value to people's lives will also add value to his own life and his children's lives. But the man who is selling products to destroy people's lives will also destroy himself and his children's lives. So, in the end the only difference is what type of karma you want to follow you and your loved ones.

Dessalines - Yes you are so right, I wish other men and women could hear what you just said right now because that's an eye opener; plus knowing this will make someone take a different path in life. Now this bible verse makes perfect sense to me, "What good does it do for a man to gain the world and lose his soul". Thank God for clarity and understanding.

Louverture- Oh yes, now that verse in the bible makes so much sense, that verse was not focusing on money but instead it focused on the choices we make to gain money.

Dessalines- Oh yes, evidently once you supply people with supplies that make them look good, feel good, and do good that same energy is coming to you like a boomerang. Next thing you know you are the most respected person like Michelle Obama or Jay-Z. You know what, I should meet that young man who owns the sandwich deli and tell him to open a franchise and level up.

Louverture- Wait you don't know him?

Dessalines - Not per say

Louverture- What? you are something else (shakes his head while laughing)

Dessalines - (laughs) But I know of him because he is "the man." He is doing great things. He came from nothing and now he has his own legit business. He is his own boss, plus he doesn't have to look over his shoulder anymore. It's all clean money that will bless him, his family, and his neighborhood. So may God bless him! May he prosper and create generational wealth!

Louverture- Amen to that! You see how when we wish good on others that same goodness will make us feel good too! That same blessing comes to us as well. Imagine if we behaved like that toward everyone, our vibration would have been to the roof. We would have been attracting lots of positive possessions, our lives and our kids' lives would have been amazing.

Dessalines - Just like God has intended, but how are you so in depth in knowledge? You are like a living philosopher like DuBois or Marcus Garvey. You are here in the hood with me and you are expounding knowledge like Solomon, you sound like you teach at Spelman or Morehouse.

Louverture- Really? Thank you for telling me that. It takes a real human being to give another human being a compliment, that's why you are my best friend. I read to understand what the author is trying to communicate to the reader. But I was blessed with great people who taught me intensive knowledge of the mind and guided me toward the right books to read. When I was a child I was dumb, in lala-land and always imagining, I never paid attention in class So I got left back couple of times too. Then when I was getting older becoming a teen I grew in my faith and started asking my creator for knowledge, understanding and wisdom. In a strange way I discovered the knowledge of the mind and I am still learning it as I go along the way. You say I am smart, but you are an intelligent woman. You make me want to do better.

Dessalines - I was not that smart either, you see how I used to struggle and barely get by in high school. I had to go to community college for 1 year so I could have gotten accepted into a university. So, when I went away to college, that's after my guidance counselor told me I wasn't the college type. I should go to beauty school or pick up some trade or something.

Louverture- Are you serious?

Dessalines- Yes but God had bigger plans for me. He gave me the best of the best professors who taught me at my level and brought me to a higher level of intelligence. I had this one professor who taught me how to analyze well, and I will never forget his first lesson in class. He strode in front of the class and drew a big circle and said this circle represents all the knowledge in the world. Then he asked each one of us to come up on the board to draw a circle that represents the amount of knowledge we think we know within the big circle he drew. One by one we lined up and drew our circles, some were as big as the one he drew and some were as small as a golf ball. After we were done, he drew a dote on the bord and said that is the amount of knowledge he knows. He dismissed us by saying, "The more you think you know, the more you don't know and only a fool thinks he knows everything." That lesson stuck with me and made me hungry for more knowledge, understanding, and wisdom. I started asking God for the same knowledge he blessed Solomon with. This professor had 11 PHDs. He is a Jesuit priest too; so, you know he is different. A true educator! I love that man, and may God bless him for what he has taught me. He didn't have to go above and beyond, but he did to help us to achieve higher and become the great intellects of our era.

Louverture- Wow he is one in a million. He made everyone realize the amount of knowledge they knew was primary to the amount of knowledge there is in the world; and now everyone in the classroom can be open to learning. But, did you know that the Jesuits used to teach the princes and princesses? And you my friend you are a true royal!

Dessalines- Yes I knew, but how do you know all this stuff who taught you these things?

Louverture- Your highness (both laugh) if you insist I communicate with my creator all the time; before I knew about all of that law of attraction and the power of positive thinking. I used to ask God to guide me. I used to ask God for help, to also bless me with wisdom like King Solomon. I didn't know what I was really asking for but look at me now; God has answered my prayers and is still answering my prayers as we speak. My God has blessed me with all that I ask him for and more. Like this African singer named Tekno said, "The same God who has blessed me is going to bless you too my friend." Just be thankful and really appreciate what you have. Ask and all will be giving to you

Dessalines - Tell me, tell me all that you know. I'm so ready to live my best life to live my dreams!

Louverture - If I start telling you some deep knowledge you won't even know what to do with yourself

Dessalines - What? What do you mean?

Louverture- I'm just playing with you (laughs) I love how your chinky eyes light up.

Dessalines - I am serious (rolls her eyes), and you are fooling around. I am really ready to learn more so I can do better for myself.

Louverture- A great mind once said, "If I tell you, you will forget. If I take my time to teach you, just maybe you will remember." But if I get you involved you will definitely learn and pass that teaching to your children's so come with me to our meeting. If the team of dreamers, like you, you might be part of our dream team family.

Dessalines - What is that? A cult?

Louverture- Really a cult? Come to this meeting with me and you will know exactly what I'm talking about. But you have to stay happy and positive. Everything starts within yourself, try your best to control your thoughts, and pay attention to how you feel and make it your personal business to feel good.

You should start reading some self-help books Devan and I used to tell you about or listen to some videos on YouTube. You are highly spiritual, so talk to our creator tonight and he will direct you to the right teacher for you. I will come pick you up tomorrow around 8pm down and I'll take you with me.

Dessalines - Wait you're leaving? Wait what videos should I watch on YouTube? What books should I read? Give me a name to start with.

Louverture- Oh You're really interested now?

Dessalines- (laugh) shut up

Louverture- I'll tell you some of the ones who helped me, great minds like Rev. Ike, Dr. Joseph Murphy, Bob Proctor, Les Brown, Steve Harvey, Abraham Hicks, Dr. Myles Munroe; those are some great minds who helped me find me plus they have some great videos on YouTube to start with. But you might find someone else like you who will help you get through your hump. Do some affirmations too. Before you do any of those things pray and meditate.

Dessalines - All right! I'll definitely do the inside job and I will be waiting for you on the porch. (both hug tightly and said their goodbyes)

Both spirits stayed connected while their human body departed to their habitation. Both were happy, both were extremely excited with a thankful heart and wanted more in life than ever before. Louverture went home to watch comedy movies, enjoy a great meal with loved ones, Do his nightly reading then meditate and pray before bed.

Meanwhile Dessalines was praying, asking God for guidance and allowing her soul to guide her to videos on YouTube that will nourish her soul and spirit. She fell on Rev. Ike, downloaded one of his free books on her phone, and watched his video on YouTube until she fell asleep. The entire night, the video was playing in her subconscious mind, she freely received his teaching without resistance.

Scene 3

The next evening Dessalines was all dressed up waiting for Louverture on her house porch. As Dessalines waited impatiently, she began to think:

I am ready!
My eyes are wide open
My ears are listening
My mouth is speechless
My brain is absorbing
My heart is racing
I am ready
To live the life of warriors
To go above and beyond without limit
To explore like Marco Polo
And live the dream like Martin Luther King
I am ready!

Finally, Louverture showed up with a book in his hand and his eyes bloody red like he just had a meeting with Mary Jay.

Dessalines - Hey, Finally
Louverture -Hey beautiful.
Dessalines - Hey, I am ready!
Louverture - For what?
Dessalines - What do you mean for what? I have been here waiting for hours while you were getting high and now you're telling me, for what?

Louverture - You see you're not ready! I have a book for you (hands book to her). Start reading it tonight and get ready.

Dessalines - (look at book) Really! Stop acting like Miyagi sensei

Louverture- I am sorry for not telling you ahead of time but, I woke up this morning and I realized it would not be fair if I took you to the meeting with me knowing you're not ready.

Dessalines- I am ready man!

I am ready!
My eyes are wide open
My ears are listening
My mouth is speechless
My brain is absorbing
My heart is racing
I am ready
To live the life of warriors
To go above and beyond without limit
To explore like Marco Polo
And live the dream like Martin Luther king
I am ready!
Louverture- You're ready?
Are you ready?
To keep your eyes wide open without blanking
To listen without judging
To keep your mouth speechless without questioning
To have your brain absorbing like a sponge without thinking
To have your heart racing without stopping
Are you ready?

To live the life of warrior without going to war
To be unlimited without going above and beyond
To be brave like Nelson Mandela
To be bold like Malcom X
Are you ready?

Dessalines - (looks confused) What? I don't get it. What do you mean?

Louverture -You see that's what I mean, you are not ready to be part of this team of Diaspora leaders. Well at least not yet!

Dessalines - Seriously, you had me waiting for you, so you can tell me I am not ready. That's not fair..

Louverture- Sometimes you have to wait in life to appreciate the fast-paced life.

Dessalines - Is that so! Was I waiting for some form of test? Was me waiting part of your lesson plan?

Louverture- I am not the one you should ask those questions. You have to answer them yourself. I am truly sorry; can we please go pass that?

Dessalines- Sure but next time send me a text okay.

Louverture- Thank you, have you been praying and meditating like we talked about yesterday?

Dessalines - No I didn't have the time to. I was watching YouTube videos. Rev. Ike had me looking at religion, God and myself differently.

Louverture – Yeah, he is really good. Matter of fact he is one of the first people I started listening to on YouTube. But meditate, do your affirmations and pray to allow your subconscious to heal you, change your paradigm, and always communicate and connect with our Creator.

Dessalines- Yes I will definitely do that. You know I am always praying but with this new knowledge my prayers will never be the same. I see it's really important to do affirmations daily, to pray, meditate, to ask and believe that it is already mine.

Louverture- I am so happy for you.

Dessalines- Me too, Tell me the truth why you are not taking me to the meeting.

Louverture- I was going to take you until I felt this desperate energy toward you. You have to clean your vibration and the best way to do that is through prayer and meditation and read the Bible too. You will be surprised how the Bible focuses on thinking positive and believing in your dreams.

Dessalines- Alright I'll do that. I guess waiting was part of my lesson and I just failed that test too (laugh)

Louverture- You are your own teacher so you get to decide if you as a student fail or not and reteach that lesson another way so you can pass it next time. The cool thing about this is that you get to teach yourself what to do, and how to do it so you can improve yourself and improve your life.

Dessalines- You are right! I will learn at my own pace, and teach at my own learning pace.

Louverture- Exactly! Anyways, I'm about to leave. I have a flight to catch in the morning, so I have to meet my team really quick and get ready for my flight.

Dessalines- You are always traveling somewhere. Where are you going this time?

Louverture- I have to go check on my businesses. I will go to China because I'm launching some new businesses and they will provide me with the packaging at the lowest price but I still want to go negotiate for a better deal. Then I am going to Haiti too, you know I export fruits and vegetables from Haiti to other countries, so I have to check on that. Plus, check on my new construction by the beach.

Dessalines - You are going to be all over the world working hard.

Louverture- Not really, I am going to be all over the world enjoying life while making money. So, I'll be hardly working and mostly having fun, that's how I look at it. Plus, I have to get things situated because I will be moving to Haiti permanently this summer, I am not just talking anymore I am taking actions toward what I believe in.

Dessalines - You right, I am proud of you, I guess I am going to be here working for someone and hardly having fun. The American dream right? Go to college, get a degree, work a 9 to 5, and take a 2-week vacation. Then you realize it's another form of slavery. Angelie Pierre was right when she said, "America takes people's dreams and give them the American Dream"

Louverture- Remember it's how you choose to look at your life and your job. If you want more out of life start changing your mind and you will see how beautiful life can be. And to be honest some people enjoy their 9 to 5. You should not be there, that's why you feel that way. You belong somewhere else. You have bigger dreams buried inside of you and you need to make some actions and unleash the lion or the eagle inside of you.

Dessalines- That's true, now I definitely see that I was not ready for the meeting and I have a lot more to learn. But I will work on myself as you travel the world and make money.

Louverture- You owe that to yourself so work on yourself and better yourself. I'll definitely see you when I get back. May the God of peace and love be with us. (Hug her and kiss her on her forehead)

Dessalines went home, uninstalled all her social media apps on her phone so she can unplug from the world to truly go within. She did all that Louverture told her to and more, she even asked her subconscious mind to guide her towards every step she made while she leaned on God's understanding. She began to appreciate the fact that she had a job as a financial analyst, in her profession of studies. Because she knew many accountant graduates who were waiting tables at a local restaurant. She started looking at life in a different perspective. She realized she was her own problem and her own solution so she went within and fixed any situation she had. Instead of blaming others she asks herself, What am I doing that causes this situation to occur? Once the answer came to her she worked at it while loving herself daily and embracing her qualities. She learned from many great teachers while reading books and watching seminars. From her understanding of those teachings she created her philosophy of greatness. Before She knew it she was in tune, tap in. Her detaching herself from the world and her flesh gives her the opportunity to attach herself to her soul and her creator. She knew she wanted to be financially independent so she can take care of herself and her mother to retire from working long hours. But she didn't really know exactly what she wanted to do so she trusted God to show her purpose in life. What God, her creator had designed for her to accomplish in this world. Every time she overheard her mother talking about the infrastructures in her country made her feel like she was the cause of the problems and her desires to move back and invest in her country grew ten times more. She knew she wanted to be a wife to a great man, a God-fearing man who will value and cherish her so she wrote all the qualities she would like in her life partner in her journal. She also wrote 10 things she was grateful for every morning in her journal after she prayed, meditated on a biblical verse and visualized. She took time during her break to recite her affirmation and visualize herself being financially independent, traveling the world, and many great things that made her feel good without any resistance.

Scene 4

Six months later, Louverture drove to Dessalines' house in the hood driving his brand-new Rolls-Royce. He honked the horn for Dessalines to see the new car, but no one came out; not one individual but the nosy neighbors. Louverture got out the car to go knock on the door.

Louverture- What's up everyone? (walks up the stairs to Dessalines house)

Neighbor- Ain't that Louverture the Haitian kid?

Louverture- Yes that's me, how y'all doing?

Neighbor- We good, we good. But your friend doesn't live out here anymore. I think they got evicted.

Louverture- What? Nahhh I don't believe that.

Neighbor- Well ask anyone in the hood they will tell you, plus the landlord came by a couple weeks ago. They were out like they were never here. Shit you coming out here on a car worth more than your friend's house. If you were a true friend you would have bought them a home and you might as well give me some bread before you leave too.

Louverture- (laugh) Thanks, I'll call Dessalines. And here some money too

Neighbor- What? Thank you, thank you, thank you. God sent you for real. I was just talking about this hair business that I want to start and all I needed was some money. (counts the money) and you gave me the exact amount I needed; God is surely good for real. May God bless you.

Louverture- Your welcome, see you around. (gets in the car and drives off while calling Dessalines on speakerphone)

Dessalines- Hello?

Louverture- Dessalines, it's Louverture. You alright? Where are you at?

Dessalines- Hey Louverture you're back! I'm happy to hear your voice. I'm home.

Louverture- What do you mean your home? I just left your house and everyone in the hood told me y'all got evicted. What is going on? I thought you were doing good. But when I didn't see you online, I just knew you took some time to find peace within like I did once. But if things were not going too well you know you could have come to me and not let it get that far. How's your mom doing? I thought that house was hers the way she used to keep that house nicely painted and extra clean.

Dessalines- You know you should not believe everything you hear. We didn't get evicted; we bought the house. Mommy is good, she is living her best life

Louverture- Alright, if you say so. I looked through the window and there was no furniture there. We have been friends since junior high in ESL class and now you can't keep it real with me. I know you are speaking things into existence, but you can tell me the truth. You will still manifest all that your heart desires but be real with me.

Dessalines- You know what talk is cheap. I will text you my house address to come over, and you can see for yourself.

Louverture- Alright thank you. (look at his phone) I receive your text. I am coming right now. (hangs up the phone and drives straight to the address. As soon as he got there called Dessalines)

Dessalines- Hey you here? Park in the driveway I'm coming out

Louverture- (gets excited) That's your house? That's really you, that's all you.

Dessalines- (walks out with the phone by her ear, pointing at Louverture's car and screaming) that's you! That's your car! I love it! That's how we doing it. Before you see my home let me take a drive down the street. (hugs each other for a long time, then gets in the Rolls-Royce).

Louverture- I'm happy to see you.

Dessalines- I am happy to see you too. I can't believe you got Rev Ike's favorite car. Business must be really good for you too.

Louverture- Yes life is great. I'm highly blessed and highly favored. But let's get out this car so you can show me that nice home you bought. I like that white Jeep Wrangler sitting on the driveway too.

Dessalines- Thanks, you're a real friend for sharing your knowledge with me and now look at us living our best life. Alright, come inside mommy is here too.

Louverture- Okay that's what's up. I haven't seen her in a while. I know she is going to talk about me not coming around.

Dessalines- Well if you say so, you know it's going to happen. (both laugh and walk in) mommy Louverture is here

Louverture- Bonsoir mommy

Maman Dessalines- Bonsoir my son, I'm happy to see you. How's the family?

Louverture- Everyone is fine thanks for asking.

Maman Dessalines- You married now?

Dessalines- Mommy really?

Maman Dessalines- Oh oh, I have all the right to ask him, you know how long I know his mom. Anyways, no wife, no kids

Louverture- No mommy I'm not married, I'm single.

Maman Dessalines- Hmmmm just like this one here. I will pray to God for you two to get married.

Dessalines- Awkward! Anyway, let me show you around the house before she starts.

Louverture- Okay mommy, let me go look at your beautiful home (follow Dessalines around the house). He is amazed to see his friend bought a beautiful 1 family home in a great neighborhood in America. He notices the large crystal chandelier while he walks to the foyer. The house was beautifully laid out with a hardwood floor in the entire house. As he walks upstairs he notices the spacious 4 bedrooms nicely furnished and the white marble tiles in the bathrooms. As he continued to follow her around he noticed the home was a smart home with the latest appliances and a beautiful granite top island in the middle of the kitchen that matched the tiles in the kitchen. The house is beautiful with lots of windows.

Dessalines- (talking to Louverture as she shows him around) Let me tell you, since you left I tried to meditate, but it wasn't easy at first. I started praying since praying was natural to me. I started talking to

God, thanking him for all that I had, thanking him for my job, my health, my annoying boss, my mom, my running water, my electricity. I was just so thankful for all of the things I had. Next thing you know more and more videos started popping up on my timeline on YouTube. Every time I finish reading one book, I'd find another one that speaks to me. The minute I saw one of Bob Proctor videos on YouTube and he mentioned the two books he read that helped him, I went online and ordered both *The Power of the Subconscious Mind* by Dr. Joseph Murphy and *Think and Grow Rich* by Napoleon Hill. I realized I was important, and it was time for me to invest in myself so I can clearly understand who I am. Where I am from. Who created me? Why am I here? What is my purpose in this world? It's like God was talking to me directly. I was opening the Bible and falling on the perfect verse I needed to hear. I'm telling you God is alive, God is real! I know it and I feel his presence.

Louverture- Amen! I am glad you took my advice. I am also glad I took others' advice when it was given to me too. Like Bob Proctor said you don't have to reinvent the wheel, you just follow the footsteps of what others did who are already successful in the same field you want to be successful in. Thanks to Andrew Carnegie who gave Napoleon Hill the task to interview successful men like himself. Now us who want success can have a map to follow, a guide to our destiny.

Dessalines- Thanks God for that man for real. You know what revolutionized me completely after you left?

Louverture- What?

Dessalines- I was thinking, it was wrong for me to want vanity or should I be focusing on helping the poor instead of wanting to be a billionaire? Until one day after I prayed to God. After I finished talking to my inner self about that same subject, I found a verse in the Bible that talked about how you will never see God's children begging. That same day I went on YouTube to watch Rev. Ike. I was directed to watch a sermon when he said, the best way to help the poor is by not becoming one of them. I froze, I was in shock. All this time I believed having too much was wrong, but it was the other way around. I want to help others, but how can I do that if I need help myself? Then before I went to bed, I accidently landed on a video of Dr. Joseph Murphy where he went to explain the verse in the Bible that talks about the love of money being the root to all evil. He said to continue reading the verse and see what it talks about, don't just stay at verse 10. So, I pulled out my Bible and opened it to 1 Timothy 6. I read the entire chapter. When I got to verse seventeen and eighteen, I said Bingo. That was the key for me, those few sentences changed my whole paradigm.

Louverture- I had the same experience a couple of years ago.

Dessalines- I was amazed, I never heard a preacher preach about the responsibilities of the ones who are rich when they read 1st Timothy 6. I now understand and believe that I serve a God who is generous. A God who gives us richly all things to enjoy! So that we can do good, and to be rich in good works ready to distribute and ready to communicate. After that my mind just changed completely! I had no more resistance, only reasons to change, so I changed completely. I started reading self-help books, doing my affirmations, doing my vision board, praying, meditating and walking around with a thankful heart. Then next thing you know my days got better and better. I finally started to use my money wisely; I used less than 50 percent of my by-weekly check. I used 10 percent for donation, I saved most of it and started an online business.

Louverture- I am glad you did. What type of business?

Dessalines- You know I love fashion, so I started an online boutique. Ideas after ideas were coming to me. I just followed anyone of them, especially the ones that made me feel alive and excited and sometimes scared too. I was just happy to be alive, happy to know what I know. My online store was getting a couple of clients a month, but I was thankful and every client meant everything to me. I was just happy to wear and sell exclusive clothes online that you couldn't find anywhere in Jersey or New York. Then one day the landlord came in and wanted to speak to mommy. She sat us down and told us she was selling most of her home in the hood. If my mom was interested she would sell it to her at a good price since she made her a billionaire

Louverture- Really! How?

Dessalines- This woman came over and told us her entire life journey, and you know my mom always has time to talk. (both laugh) She told us how she came over on a boat from Italy in the 1950's with her brother. They were two teenagers who had to make the sacrifice so their family could live a better life. When they got off the boat

Louverture- Wait, they didn't go to immigration? They didn't have to pay for a visa?

Dessalines- Nope not like us black immigrants, she said all they needed was an address to someone's home so they didn't have to sleep on the street and of course the immigration laws were not strict until the Latin and Black immigrants started migrating to the US.

Louverture- Of course.

Dessalines- So once her and her brother came to America they stayed with a family member and worked so they could bring the rest of their family over. She didn't finish high school; she worked at a farm in Jersey picking blueberries, just like many immigrants are doing today. She said they paid her 50 cents for each basket she filled up and she used to make 3 to 4 dollars a day. With that money she saved up. Plus, her brother's money, they put it together and brought their parents and siblings over to America. After that, she moved to New York City to work in the factories making clothes for all the big-name brands and department stores. All 6 of them lived in a one-bedroom apartment in the city and shared the bills and saved up their money to be able to live the American dream. At eighteen she married a hard-working Italian man from the same town as her. She said they were like the perfect team. He paid the bills; she saved her money and saved the extras he gave her for groceries. Then when the money was a good amount, she told her husband let's buy a house. He thought she was crazy until she showed him all the money she has been saving up under their mattress. They paid the house in cash and had money to buy nice furniture too.

Louverture- Was that the house you and your mom was renting?

Dessalines- Yes! They lived there and raised their children and continued bringing families over. Each family who migrated to America came and stayed in her home, paying her a little each month once they started working, until they got on their feet and moved out to make space for their other families. With the money she took from her family members she paid their bills, fed the families, and she used her and her husband's money to bring more families to America. She said, "It was like a way of life, every immigrant did it. Their neighbors from Irish, Germany, Slovenia, Russia, you know all the other European countries did the same thing. That was their goal, to make America their home and they did! So, they didn't have a reason to go back since all their loved ones were in America. They became Americans, they were proud to call themselves Americans too, speaking only English to their children who were now true Americans with no accents." After she accomplished that mission her and her husband saved up and built themselves a home in south Jersey. They lived there with their children and had some family members stay at their 2-family home in north Jersey.

Louverture- Wait, is that the same home you and your mom lived in?

Dessalines- Yes, and once every family was out of her house she got into the real-estate business and she rented my mom the bottom floor and another family the top floor. My mom always paid on time, so she saved every penny my mom was giving her and went to the bank, got a loan, and brought 4 more homes in the same neighborhood and rented them out. She paid the loan with the money she received from the other tenants, but she managed to save my mom money and continue to buy more properties after properties. Her husband was a hard worker, but she was a hustler with a clear vision. She provided people in the hoods with homes and they paid her good money; she even took people with Section 8 too. She saved all her money and started buying buildings after buildings and even plazas too. She accomplished all of that in less than 10 years.

Louverture- Wow

Dessalines- Can you believe this little immigrant lady who didn't even know how to speak English, didn't finish high school, owns over 50 plazas and apartment buildings? Imagine what we can accomplish at her age. Her and her husband are very successful because of her. She was never comfortable or satisfied so now they own blocks after blocks. They made billions in the same hood black people are running away from.

Louverture- That's a boss lady for fact!

Dessalines- Yes! She said she was aiming for the American dream, but she surpassed it and landed in the same bracket as Carnegie.

Louverture- Wait, the house you lived in was the first home her and her husband purchased since they came to America with the factory money. And they lived there for over ten years then rented it to your mom, who always paid her rent on time and kept her house super clean. So, while your mom was paying them rent, she was saving that money, paid off their mortgage payment, she bought a couple more homes and rented them to other families. So that's what they did, they flipped their money from houses until they ended up owning several blocks and retail spaces for rent, and next thing you know they became billionaires just like that. They made all that money from the hood, they are geniuses!

Dessalines- Yes just like that! That's the beauty and strength of a powerful couple,

Louverture- Yes! They became billionaires off those raggedy homes in the hood. When people saw trouble, they saw opportunities

Dessalines- Yeah she said that too. She told my mom that God told her to sell her their first home. So, she came over and did just that.

Louverture- You see, since your vibration was high, you created opportunities for you and your mom.

Dessalines- I sure did. And you know what? I barely made 5 sales of my online business then. But I was thankful, and I was happy for every check I received from my job. Plus, I was happy for my mom who allowed me to stay rent free in her home. Then I stumbled on this Young man who helps people fix their credit so they can be able to get business loans, and every type of loan you can think of. So, I contacted him, and I used my income from work to fix my credit.

Louverture- That's great, you see the minute you are thankful and appreciate all that you have, more ideas to improve your life will start coming your way.

Dessalines - You are right about that but going back to my mom and our landlord story. You would not believe how much she sold my mom the house for. Plus, she told her where to go to apply for a mortgage and how she can get 10 thousand since my mom was a first home buyer.

Louverture- For how much?

Dessalines- For 50 thousand U.S Dollars!

Louverture- Kisa? 50 thousand for the 2 family homes, wow! That's God, God did that. Look at God. Look how he blesses you. I'm happy for you. Keep doing your thing, keep being thankful and God will just continue to bless you more and more.

Dessalines- Thank you, thank you. Now we are living in this beautiful home while the house in the hood is paying for our mortgage, bills and taxes. I am so thankful for this opportunity and I want to continue to buy properties just like the Italian lady did.

Louverture- You should, I believe you were supposed to do that too. You're already an accountant and you might as well start working for yourself.

Dessalines- Yes I am; I am so thankful to have you as a friend; I pray for you every day. But how are you driving a Rolls-Royce in your 30's? You are already making money like that? I know you was rich, but I didn't know you was rich rich

Louverture- I just became rich, rich, so I bought myself a rich, rich car. That makes me feel good, but you know when I was traveling, I was handling businesses while enjoying life. All my businesses tripled without me making any efforts. Plus, I purchased 60 more organic farms in Haiti than the ones you knew about. The best part, I landed a deal with the number one organic food supplier in Europe and Canada. That deal made me a billionaire, so I treated myself to one of Rev. Ike's favorite cars. But I am in town for a couple of days, you ready to come to that meeting with me.

Dessalines- I am so proud of you! Of course, when is the next meeting?

Louverture- It's tomorrow morning

Dessalines-Oh great, I am going to request a personal day right now. (pulls up phone to email HR)

Louverture- Wait, you still work at that place?

Dessalines- Of course. I will quit when I'm rich just like you.

Louverture- Oh okay, do what works for you. But before I leave, one thing I can tell you from my experience is that, whatever you sell or do, make sure it is adding value to people's lives. Because that's when the big bucks start rolling in trust me, you see my car out your driveway.

Dessalines- (both laugh) You are right about that, that's why any businessmen who are intentionally selling toxic to society end up being toxic and looking toxic. If they don't change their ways their children end up paying for their malicious ways.

Louverture- Remember when I used to sell drugs back in my ignorant day. I became reckless and toxic, that wicked business never got me nowhere, plus I can't remember what I did with that dirty money. That fast life can't get you nowhere but in prison or six feet under.

Dessalines- For real, but look at you now you're a changed man. I am proud of you. You are driving a half a million-dollar car, you have business all over the world, plus everyone respects you. You're a real one and I know others who are coming home will be just like you. All about their businesses.

Louverture- Yes, and America will be surprised to see their unwanted children at the top sitting right and eating right just like me. But knowing you I will be here all night; I am going to leave before we get on to another topic. I'll text you the address in the morning

Dessalines- Knowing me, really (both laugh) alright, but make sure to say buy to my mom before you leave. You know how Haitian parents can be very sensitive.

Louverture- Of course. Mommy, mâle oui

Maman Dessalines- Déjà, wait I want to talk to you really quick

Dessalines- Here you go (both laugh) (whispers) you here for another 5 hours go take a seat

Louverture- Ok mommy. Congratulations on your homes

Maman Dessalines- Thank you my son. You see how God is good and merciful to me. If I tell you my story (points at her chest) you will know for fact that God is alive, and he is a loving and merciful God

Dessalines- Mommy, he has to go

Louverture- It's okay I have time.

Maman Dessalines- You know I am an immigrant, but I don't think you know how I made my journey to this country. How I sacrificed all I had to live in the land of the free. You know I was one of the first ones who came on a boat from Haiti.

Louverture- really

Maman Dessalines- You know I worked for a company named Sunoco in the 1980's in Haiti. I was a single mother and my baby was just 1 years old. 6 months into the job the company shut down and decided to go to China or Dominican Republic because there were political problems, you know civil war. That was the time Duvalier lost power and everything we had changed for the worst. I was sixteen years old and making good money at the time. I even bought a piece of land after a month of working there. I was getting ready to build my little house until they told us one Monday morning that the company was closing. Can you imagine a single mom who needs to buy milk and diapers for their child? Can you imagine going into work knowing you have it all together then they told you sorry we are closing this is our last week?

Louverture- What? that's crazy

Maman Dessalines-Oh yes, very crazy and you know what there was no unemployment, no welfare, no child support, no system in place to help us. I had two choices, the first one was to go back to my village with a child without a dad and my last check to live there to suffer with my baby girl. Or go back to my village, leave my baby behind, and take my last check to pay for that boat trip that my co-workers were organizing. Everything in me told me to do it; I was fearless. I knew I was going to make it alive even though I knew there was a fifty percent chance of me dying in the middle of the Atlantic Ocean. I trusted God and my God delivered, my God came through. You know it was over 150 of us on that boat, sleepless night with no life saver; plus, I didn't even know how to swim.

Louverture- Are you serious?

Maman Dessalines- Can you imagine? I held on to that boat and I held on to God tighter. I saw people falling out of the boat dying of hunger or thirst, and the captain dropping them off like they were pieces of trash. ten of my good friends died off that boat (tears come down her eyes) but I couldn't cry, I was fighting for my life and my baby's life.

Dessalines- Mommy, it's okay to cry.

Maman Dessalines- (Wipe her tears) Can you tell a soldier to cry at a bottle field?

Louverture- That's true.

Maman Dessalines- But I continued praying, and you know what? I didn't eat anything on that boat I fasted the whole time. I prayed and sipped a little bit of water throughout the journey. When we finally reached Cuba, our boat crashed. The Cuban government offered us to stay and a place to live and jobs just like the Haitians offered the Black

American slaves when they were running for their freedom.

Louverture- Wow, why didn't you stay?

Maman Dessalines- I trusted God. If I stayed, I would have doubted him. I believed he was going to take me to America, and when 20 of my co-workers stayed, I said I am going to America. The Cubans fixed our boat and I got on and said I am going to America and God is my captain. I had faith that could move mountains and an empty gallon of water to help me float. They told us in the middle of the ocean between Cuba and Miami there was a leman, you know a tornado under the water. We had a twenty percent chance of making it.

Louverture- What's that?

Dessalines- The Bermuda triangle

Toussaint- Oh okay, that's a danger zone

Maman Dessalines- Yes, and you know what? I said to the Cubans, well God got us and he is the eighty percent chance so that makes it 100% percent chance of surviving. I didn't eat a thing in Cuba either. I only drank water. I said to myself if Jesus and his disciples fasted for 40 days and they were fine I too can fast until I made it to the land of the free. You know when we reached the area that they told us we only had a twenty percent chance of surviving. The captain told us to hold on to the boat and pray.

Louverture- What? What did you do?

Dessalines- My child I am telling you, only if he knew I was already praying and thanking God for a safe journey. You know what happened that day? God calmed the ocean! There were no big waves.

The ocean was calm like never before and that day I knew that my God is a great God, my God, is alive and will always answer my prayers. We got to the shore of Miami at midnight, there was not one there it was pitch black. And I looked to my left and my right, everyone I personally knew died on that boat. It was 80 of us who stepped foot to the land of the free. 20 of us stayed behind and 55 of us died in the ocean. I, a 16-year-old girl with a child to feed, made it by God's grace. All my friends died in that ocean without no proper burial, with no one to tell their family they didn't make it. I had nowhere to stay but I walked out that water like I had a family member in America.

Louverture- Wait, you left Haiti knowing you didn't have no one in America?

Maman Dessalines- My son, I had God! (she tilts her head back leaning on the couch while tears run down her cheeks) I did, I did. My friends Suzzete, Janine, Marise, Sandra, Polinne, Therese, Sandrine, Georgette, Polene, Janette, Claudette, Marie, Janne, Edline, Anne; Oh, Jesus They all died in the ocean, and they all promise me a place to stay with their family members. They all died without a proper burial, they all died leaving children behind. Leaving parents behind who were hopping on their call. (scream) Oh Jesus De Nazarete! (Maman Dessalines wipes her tears and walks to the bathroom sobbing)

Louverture- (whispers to Dessalines) Did you know this story?

Dessalines- No, not with all those details.

Louverture- Are you serious?

Maman Dessalines walks back to the living room holding a photo album in her hand.. She sits down and she opens the photo album.

Maman Dessalines- Those are all the children my friends left behind. They became my responsibility; they became my children. I made sure all of them finished high school and graduated college. All eighteen of them are professionals now, five of them are doctors, four are lawyers, six are accountants and the other 3 are business owners.

Dessalines- What? I thought they were my cousin's mommy.

Maman Dessalines- No my love. I made it my personal business to find each one of them and take care of them like they were my family. Just like their mom used to look after me when I was a young girl working at the factory.

Louverture- That's why God bless you with this beautiful home.

Dessalines- Plus that big mansion you build in Haiti and the rental property we have.

Maman Dessalines- I am thankful for all that God bless me with, but what human being would have the heart to watch their friends died in the middle of the ocean and not take care of their love ones

Louverture- You will be surprised not everyone has a pure heart like yours

Dessalines- Yes mommy, but what happened that night you first came to America? Where did you sleep?

Maman Dessalines- Let me tell you how God is good to me. That night I watched everyone who was on the boat with me one by one used a pay phone and called family members and left. I had no one but God and I said to God that night, "Yahweh if you want me to experience sleeping on the street tonight, I am fine with that. Thank you for allowing me to make it safe, to reach America the land of dreamers. The land of opportunities where every dream comes true." I stayed on the floor watching cars pull up and Haitians running in while the rest of us hid behind a bush. Each family member paid the captain and took off like they never met. But I sat there waiting on God, thanking him for allowing me to make it through my journey. I was pleased to be sitting on the American soil and knowing that my life will only get better after this. My daughter will be able to live the American dream and my God will lift our heads high. When the sun started to rise the captain said to me, "Where are your people?" I told him they all died in the ocean. He was shocked and said you have no one in America. I shook my head and said I only have God. He said you're a crazy little girl and said come with me. He took me to this big house in Miami where many other Haitians rent a place to sleep and told me I will be fine.

Louverture- You were brave for a sixteen-year-old girl.

Maman Dessalines- I had to be brave, experience will turn you into someone you never thought you were capable of being.

Louverture- You are right about that!

Dessalines- You know the next morning the captain told me it's because of my faith we made it to America. I didn't have to pay him, he told me he watched me pray, he knew I was fasting. He said, he saw hope in my eyes when all my friends were afraid. He continued by saying my faith saved all of us and this was his 10th and last time doing this journey. The spirits around me saved us and now he needs to go pray to God. I made him see that God is alive, after all his journeys and saw hundreds of people die in the Atlantic oceans, he doubted God, but this journey was different. A child made him see that God is there to help us, we only have to believe and hold on to that faith!

Dessalines- Wow mommy, why have you never told me that? I never knew all of that happened to you, wow you should share your story with the rest of the world

Maman Dessalines - (point at herself) me, I am an immigrant. I never finished high school and my English is bad, who would want to hear my story? Americans can't even understand me when I speak; it's best if I don't speak. You who have a college degree, can tell my story for me? That's why I brought you here, you can tell people our struggle and the sacrifices we made to come here. Remember to always tell them how God took us out, how God protected us and saved us. You and Toussaint and every child of immigrants should tell their parents' journey. Like I tell you my ancestor's stories.

Louverture- Wow I respect you and everyone who made that journey. But mommy everyone have a story to tell, everyone should speak up and tell their truth

Maman Dessalines- Thank you my son, but not me.

Dessalines- Maman, what happened after that night?

Maman Dessalines - The next day I ate everything I could find until I had diarrhea (laughs). My children, you know that big house the captain took me to was his. Later I found out he had 5 houses like that, plus his own home with his wife and kids. He told the lady who was running the house I can stay there for 6 months without paying rent. I said thank you, but where can I go for work? I have a 1-year old child who needs to be fed. The day after I went to the tomato plantation. I worked there for 2 years and saved my money for my papers even if I knew I had no relatives to file for me.

Dessalines- Mommy you acted out of faith.

Maman Dessalines- Yes my child, when Chaves the Mexican King fought for his people in the farms to have green cards, he fought for every immigrant who was working like slaves on that land. He didn't see different skin colors or nationalities, but he saw human beings who didn't have a voice. Once again God answered my prayers. I believed that I would have my paper, so I was saving my money for it. I was one of the first ones to fill out for the farmer's working permit and after, a green card. When some of my friends I met at the farm were moving to New York for better jobs, I said I'm going too. That was the first time I flew on a plane from Miami to JFK airport. The 6 of us were young women but I was younger than all of them. We all stayed in someone's sister's basement and each one of us left one by one after we brought our children over. I was one of the last ones to leave that basement and I didn't unite with my child until she was twelve years old.

Louverture- Wow, that's the age I was when I met my mom too.

Maman Dessalines- That was hard; (tears roll down her eyes) can you imagine what that felt like as a mom to leave your only child behind and to unite with that child when they are almost an adult? I missed out on a lot of things, my baby getting her first tooth, my baby learning how to walk, my baby's first day of school, my baby learning how to read, my baby getting in trouble in school, my baby picture days, my baby kindergarten graduation, my baby's birthdays; all of those things I cannot replace.

Dessalines- (crying) All of those memories I had to face and no shoulder to cry on, because society told me I was lucky to have a mother who sacrifice so much for me. But they felt to realize that "I am the lamb, I am the sacrifice" (hide her face to cry)

Maman Dessalines- You had people, but I know you needed your mommy, she needed to hear my voice telling her that's my girl. If only people knew what us, women and children who are separated for a better life face. If only they knew half of our stories. What we deal with and how we can't ever replace those precious moments. (Dessalines and mom start crying). That was the sacrifice I had to make, and I made my sacrifice so we can live in America, the land of the free, the land of opportunities (looks at her daughter).

Louverture- wow (fighting for the tears not to come down)

Maman Dessalines- My father died behind my back, I couldn't be there to speak at his funeral, to bury him. My sibling got married and had kids behind my back. I lived a life of loneliness, of solitude and I never one day felt lonely because God was always with me, God always watched over me. God blessed me and saved me and my only child. Now we are rich in America, (puts up both hands like she was reaching for the sky and looking up to the heavens) Thank you Jesus Christ! Can you believe someone like me who came with an empty gallon of water and a pair of sneakers tied around my neck is a homeowner in the number one country: in America! I did it all with God's mercy. My child is a college graduate, my child works and has a big office at one of the big buildings downtown where I used to clean the bathrooms and empty out the garbage cans in the offices. Imagine what the two of you can do if you put all your faith in God! Imagine what your kids can do? Just imagine how far you can go. Merci Jesus, Merci Jesus.

Louverture- Amen !

Maman Dessalines- Yes amen, alleluya. Before I let you go, you know what is my last dream? What I want for Jesusla and the boat people's children, the immigrants to do? To open businesses, buy properties, invest in real estates and in anything that they see will profit them Just like the Italians did. You know I went to Haiti last year and visited the factory I used to work at. No one was there, not one soul. It is empty waiting for our children to re-open it, to create jobs for those who are starving. I want every immigrant child who made the same sacrifice like Jesula and I did, the ones who ran out of the country when Haiti was getting worse to run back. The way America is moving they don't want us immigrants to be here anymore. They are tired of us and I understand. I mean I love my country Haiti; I am a nationalist. I always was, even if misery and a lack of a job had forced me out. I don't feel comfortable when I go to my country and see some of the businesses are owned by foreigners and they are paying the Haitians 40 cents a day. It makes me want to tell all the rich diasporas, let's revolt and go back and make our shit hole country great like it was before the US. invasion.

Louverture- Wait, America invaded Haiti?

Maman Dessalines- Yes my son, in 1915. My grandmother told me stories of those years of exploitation.

Dessalines- what? I can't believe it, and now this country wants to act like we are exploiting them.

Maman Dessalines- That's the consequences you have to pay when you are not in your country. One advice my mother gave me when I was a child running in and out of people's homes was to know when to walk away when you are not wanted in someone's home. That is called dignity!

Louverture- yes!

Maman Dessalines- In the 80's and 90's even the 2000's, our country couldn't offer us anything. But we wanted better lives so we made the sacrifice to come here by boat, by plane, by train some of us cross the borders by foot just like the Mexicans did. But we fail to tell our children our stories. I want you guys and all of your friends who came here young and had every opportunity that America could offer to make a sacrifice and trust God like I did. God didn't choose you out of millions to come to America and build the American empire. Your purpose was to come learn, make money and go build your own empire so we can have a well-balanced world.

Dessalines- Yeah

Maman Haiti- Yea, You kids are immigrants just like me but you are not embarrassed when the American people say why your country is so poor? My answer is this; the immigrants are getting too comfortable. They forgot why God choose them to come to the number 1 empire, they forgot that they have to go back to their country of origin and open big businesses and create jobs so people don't have to make the journey like I did, So people don't have to die like my friends from work died because they had no jobs no hope (tears rolling down her cheeks).

Dessalines- Mommy I understand, but not everyone wants to go back and do all of the great things you are talking about.

Maman Dessalines- (wipe her tears) It is not what you want but what God had plans for you. Why do you think it is more uncomfortable to live in America? Why do you think they keep insulting us? Why do you have to fight to stay where you are unwanted? Don't you trust God and the plans he has for you to make you prosper and flourish in your own land? Fok the American Dream, pa gen lot

Louverture- When you don't want to move God will make you uncomfortable so you have to move.

Maman Dessalines- Yes, it is because God plans is bigger than you. Many young diaspora don't know that life is about sacrifices and trusting God while allowing God to use them like a precious vessel. We love to say 1804 but are we continuing the 1804 legacy, It is important for us children of warriors to continue what our ancestors started and rebuild our own country if not we will never be at peace in a stranger lands because there are chaos in our own land

Dessalines- Mommy I want to do all the great things you are talking about. Some of us are already doing it but do you know how many of us came to this country when we were kids? It has to be millions of us. Do you think it is a collective purpose to go back home and create great infrastructures?

Maman Dessalines- I don't know what God has planned for everyone, but if any of us feel uncomfortable or enrage every time we hear these words the Black countries who took their independence are the poorest country in the world then you are part of God's collective plan.

Louverture- Mommy I agree with you 100 percent, if someone feels uncomfortable it is because God assigned them to be part of something great. People love to say If I was around doing this revolution, doing slavery time I would have done this or that, But what are you doing now? What are you doing in this revolution? Will your name be in the history books or will you be able to look your kids in the eyes and said I was part of something great? Or will depression from not expressing yourself doing this worldly revolution silent you for life?

Maman Dessalines- I read somewhere it said, the greater is sacrifice the greater is the gain! When I think about the sacrifices I made to come to America, the sacrifices my daughter had to face, I know there is more to come.

Louverture- You know what I am always telling Dessalines that.

Maman Dessalines- (shakes her head) My child, Jesusla Dessalines can be stubborn at times, and she wonder why she is not married yet

Dessalines- Really mommy

Louverture- Well mommy some guy will love her and her stubbornness.

Maman Dessalines- Oh yea, Speak for yourself my son.

Dessalines- Okay, it's time for you to go right Louverture? Don't you have somewhere to go? Mom it's almost time for your Bible study, it's best if you go before it's too late

Maman Dessalines- Oh thank you. I am sitting here talking with you two and I didn't see the time flying. But Jesusla give your friend here something to eat okay. My son, come to see me again, we have to continue our conversation. Before I forget, when you kids tell my story remember to not tell them my real age. (everyone laughs)

Louverture- Okay mommy

Maman Dessalines walked to her room 15 minutes later she walked out with a church hat in her head and a Bible in her hand. She kisses both Dessalines and Louverture while she proceeds to the car with her Bible under her arm.

Dessalines- I'm telling you Haitian parents never want you to date but as soon as you turn 25 with a college degree they want you to get married like the person is going to fall down the sky and straight to your feet. They want you to have it all. I'm telling you. But don't mind her.

Louverture- I'm used to it; you know my mom is worse when you come over. But I do admire your stubborn self.

Dessalines- (looks at Toussaint as she makes her way to the kitchen) shut up, you want something to eat for real? Or I'll tell my mom you ate already.

Louverture- (following Dessalines to the kitchen) ooo tanpri! I will eat, you know how Haitian be extremely sensitive when you don't want to eat at their house (both laugh)

Dessalines- It's not that serious (laughs as she starts putting some food on the plate for Toussaint)

Louverture- You know what Jesusla, your mom was right about a lot of things. Now I have to go ask my mom questions about her journey to America

Dessalines- You should, but don't call me that, you know I hate my first name Dieudoner Louverture!

Louverture- Alright (laughs) what were our parents thinking when they named us for real.

Dessalines- You know what my mom told me? When my dad ran away when she was 6 months pregnant with me she said it's okay Jesus is here! Jesus la! get it and that's how she named me Jesusla

Louverture- Really? That's cute. Well as for me, you know my mom couldn't have kids for many years and my dad's family kept humiliating her and one day she said God is the one who gave Dieu donne. Next month she was pregnant with me and called me Dieudonner (both laugh)

Dessalines- I'm telling you our parent's faith is so strong and powerful. I am amazed at my mom making her journey on a banana boat at 16 years old. I never heard something like this before and I am proud of my mom for that. If she did all that without knowing how to even speak a word of English, imagine what we can do with all the knowledge we have. She just gave me extra strength right now and I believe that I can do anything, and Jesus is here, just like my name Jesusla. (she brings the food to Toussaint)

Louverture- Yes Jesusla. I love how you are serving your man.

Dessalines- My man

Louverture- Yes Jesusla Dessalines, I am falling in love with you and I don't see myself with no one else but you. You know me more than anyone else. You knew me when I was broke at my lowest point, and I had many women as we all know but now I only feel the need for you. I can't see myself without you. You are my best friend, you have a

127

good spirit, you have your mind right plus you know how to cook. Jesusla females like you are hard to find, you're the true definition of a complete woman.

Dessalines- What did I tell you about that? Don't call me by my government name Dieudonner! This is my mom's house too so have some respect! Anyways when is that meeting? You know I have been thinking about what my mom said, I am going to invest in Haiti and open my businesses in Haiti. After all it's cheaper to live in the Caribbean plus the climate is wonderful. I'm ready to live that island life now.

Louverture- Really? You are going to act like you didn't hear me? Why Haitian women are so extra.

Dessalines- Then get yourself an American so you can eat fried chicken and black rice all day

Louverture- You have jokes (laugh) You know I make the best black rice.

Dessalines- Yes I do! Plus, Black American make the best fried chicken so you are on the perfect direction. Let me know when you find your Laquisha

Louverture- Really? You know how long ago I stopped talking to her and you are going to bring up her name out of all people

Dessalines- Yes your list of names are so long I can't even count

Louverture- (walked up to Jesusla and whispers in her ears) I love you!

Dessalines- (step back while looking Toussaint in the eyes speechless and in shock)

Louverture- That was my past, please don't look at me for the person I was in my reckless days. I paid for my past already. Please see me as the growing man that I am today! Can you please do that Jesusla Dessalines?

Dessalines- (shakes her head) Yes, but it's not you

Louverture- What? You don't love me?

Dessalines- Sorry but...

Louverture- It is okay I will leave. I'm sorry

Dessalines- - Wait! I do! But, I am afraid.

Louverturer- You love me, that's all that matters! Please do not let fear control our destiny. You and I both know the power of words. Please love do not speak fear into our relationship

Dessalines- But this is different. This is personal, it is not the same.

Louverture- Please let go and let God and you will see we were made for each other.

Dessalines- Can I trust you with my heart?

Louverture- Please just give it a try. Let's take things slow so you can build trust. I know better; therefore, I will do better. I value you like I value my own life.

Dessalines- (stares into Toussaint eyes) I don't know.

Louverture- It is you that I want Jesusla your sexy self, your pretty dark skin, your brilliant mind and your beautiful soul

As Jesusla Dessalines turned around to say something, Louverture grabbed her and tongue kissed her. He grabbed her softly and wrapped her

in his arms. For years he prayed to God for her and finally his prayers were answered. At that moment, Maman Dessalines walked in the house and headed straight to the kitchen

Maman Dessalines- Jesusla, I forgot my Bible study notebook. (she stood in shock looking at her daughter and Louverture) OOOO just like that in my house

Louverture- Oh sorry, it's time for me to leave good night (runs out the house and drove off)

Maman Dessalines- That's your boyfriend Jesusla?

Dessalines- No mommy

Maman Dessalines- What do you mean it's not your boyfriend? I find you having sex with him in my kitchen. So, what is it sex friend? I didn't raise a sex friend! I raised a wife. Tell your vagabond friend to not come here if all he wants is a prostitute!

Dessalines- Mommy really, it was only a kiss we had full clothes on. He told me he was in love with me and grabbed me by the neck and kissed me.

Maman Dessalines- Oh excuse me, by the neck, that's where your neck is now (pointing at Jesusla behind) so you love him too

Dessalines- I don't know?

Maman Dessalines- I don't know. You better know Jesusla (grab her notebook walks out to go to church with her Bible study notebook in her hand while whispering) Merci Jesus. Thank you Jesus Christ!

Dessalines- (still in shock) Oh Lord why?

She walks upstairs to her room. As she lay on her bed her phone rang. She quickly picks it up.

Dessalines- Hello

Toussaint- Hey Jesusla, I am sorry. I know how Haitians moms are strict on their daughters. Damn I'm sorry. I thought she was gone, now she is going to think of me as a vagabond. I hope she is not mad at you or me.

Dessalines- It's okay Dieudonner. I am tired, I'll talk to you in the morning. I have to go set my mind before I fall asleep

Louverture- This early it's only 7 pm. Remember the meeting is tomorrow morning. I'll meet you there and after I'll come over and talk to your mom if that is okay with you

Dessalines- Okay good night

Louverture- Wait Jesusla, it's okay for me to be your man. Our ancestors will finally unite. You know I'm the great grandchild of Toussaint Louverture. You're the great grandchild of Jean Jacque Dessalines. We will create a great force, I love you girl

Dessalines- BYE Dieudonner. I will talk to you in the morning. I didn't say I want to be with you yet.

Louverture- Yet, okay. I can live with that, good night. Mwen renmenw, Je t'aime

Dessalines- bye

She hangs up her phone, prays, and does her affirmations before going to bed. While lying in bed

she could not sleep, the thought of how Louverture kissing her dawned on her. She was scared and didn't know what to do. She loved him as a friend but never knew if her feelings were that deep and that strong for him until that kiss. That one kiss opens her eyes and awakens her love that has been buried inside of her. Emotions were pouring in; she never felt an emotion so strong before and instead of fighting it she has to allow it.

Scene 5

The next morning both of them are up early doing their morning routine. And preparing for the meeting.

(Phone rings)

Louverture- Good morning my love. I hope you had a good night's sleep. I sent you the address to the place. Make sure you are here early. I'll be there on time, I just have to make some errands too

Dessalines- Good morning to you too.

Louverture- what time does your mom get home from work today?

Dessalines- She doesn't work anyone, she quit 3 weeks ago, she is getting ready to go to Haiti next week.

Louverture- that's great I didn't know that.

Dessalines- Yeah since our rental property is paying our bills it didn't make sense for her to work anymore

Louverture- Ok, well we will talk more later ok, I am looking forward to seeing your pretty face.

Dessalines- See you later, bey. (hang up the phone)

When it was time, Dessalines got dressed to look her best and went to the meeting. As soon as she got there she called Toussaint.

Dessalines- Hey I'm outside

Louverture- Okay stay right there. I'll come get you outside love

Dessalines- You need to stop, my future husband may be in the meeting, please don't ruin it for me

Louverture- You're right, I am in the meeting

Dessalines- bye (hangs up the phone)

Louverture (yells) hey Jesusla park right here, there is no more parking available so park right there. (starts running toward the car)

Louverture opens the door and both of them walk in as a power couple. The room was full of great minds, full of diversity, full of leaders in all different types of fields. It looked like a meeting at the United Nations but without the boring suits and ties. There were 80 different languages spoken in the room. Everyone in that room identified their God given gift and used it to their full human potential.

Mentor- Good morning all. I'm glad we were able to make it today. It's a beautiful day to be alive, it's a beautiful day to live our dreams and make things happen for ourselves by using our God given talents. I am proud to be among all of my dreamers who stepped out their comfort zone and followed their true-life callings. That's why we are the dreamers; we are living our ancestors' wildest dreams. I will be short today but as you all know I can talk but I'll be quick. To begin, welcome all the new faces to our team. We are a family, we are a community, we are a nation. So, before you leave today, exchange contact information with everyone because we are forming a team that will spread out and help each other grow and expand true love and unity. In order to be great, we have to make sacrifices, we have to sleep less hours until we reach our goals. For the ones who still have a 9 to 5 you will have to do that. Many great leaders did it, Steve Harvey did, that's why he is where he is today. Like Les Brown said, "You have to do the things that others won't do today so you can have the things others won't have in the future." By the way, I am not saying for you to compete with other people. I am saying for you to get up early when you are normally sleeping. Work on your God given talents instead of watching T.V. Listen to self-motivation instead of gossiping with friends and loved ones. Build that relationship with your creator. Trust me, life will only get sweeter by the minute. If God is on our side no one can be against us! The floor is open ladies and gentlemen.

Anakarona- Good morning all. As we know, the rest of the world may not know that immigrants have it hard. But us immigrants or children of immigrants took every bit of hardness that was thrown at us and made something great out of it. We see what is happening on the borders. We see the suffering of children and mothers and fathers. We see how America can be cold and bitter like Chicago in the winter. But we also know that America can be sweet and warm like California weather. Instead of focusing on America with immigrants, let's raise our vibration and continue to pray and make things happen for us diaspora who came from all parts of the world searching for peace, searching for opportunities, searching for a better life. And like Akon said, it's no man land

Voltaire- Who's Akon?

Lumumba- Really Voltaire?

Voltaire- What? I like what she said. It is no man's land. So, I want to know who said it.

Mentor- Come guys we are not here for that. Today is an important meeting. Voltaire please don't pay attention to Lumumba; he is always teasing you.

Marley- Voltaire, Akon is who we should look up to; he is the king in Africa right now. He is a diaspora just like us who lived in America at a young age just like us. He was locked up in the corrupt system and took his oppression and became a great artist and businessman. Now he is giving the whole continent of Africa electricity. Plus, he have a key to Jersey City

Hike- Okay I know exactly who you are talking about. He is a billionaire too. That's a smart man, I love to hear about people like me making money.

Angelou- Yes he is someone we all should look up too. But can someone please tell the agenda of this meeting and who called for this meeting?

Louverture- Once everyone gets here we can start this meeting. It's very important that we discuss everything together.

Biko- This meeting was scheduled for 10 am now it's 10 :15. We should start on time.

Mentor- You know you're right let's start so we can finish on time. Can someone please record as we start.

Gandhi- I would like for everyone to turn off their phones so we can start our meditation and prayer. Except for the ones who are recording.

As they were meditating, the rest of the gang came in and joined in to meditate and pray. This was an interesting group of individuals, different shades of color from different walks of life and many different languages in one tiny room in Jersey City New Jersey, the most diverse city in the world. But all had one comment goal, one ideology "f*ck the American dream".

Everyone here were leaders, and everyone were followers. Each of them knew when it was their time to lead and follow, a day like today everyone had to lead, everyone had to decide and act. Their lives depended on this meeting. Today is the day that will change their entire destiny.

Senghor- (stands up tall) Thank you everyone for coming and thank you Gandhi for leading us into a peaceful state. We are one, we are equal, we are plural, we are love. That's why I love me, I love you, I am you and you are me. Thank you... (sits down)

Mentor- The Queen Mia Angelo stated many years ago in her masterpiece Poem, "Cage Bird". All of us are familiar with her works so I do not need to recite it today. Mia Angelo expresses why the caged bird sings, how the cage bird is in bondage in a cage dreaming, witching he can be like the free bird who dares to claim the sky. Us this

generation we are here to tell our Queen Mai Angelo
All cages doors have been unlocked!
All cages doors are now open wide!
All birds are free!
We have broken down the narrow cages!
We quickly surpass the broken cage bars!
Our wings are spread!
Our feet are free!
We think of another breeze, a positive breeze my Queen Maya Angelo!
We know the sky is our starting point!
Now we stand tall!
Fly high!
Live our dreams.
As we sing of the freedom we live!
Everyone- (stand tall and applaud while shouting) Yes yes we are free!
Harrison- Yeah and that's how God intended for us to live, free, free to travel and live wherever we want in this world.
Rodney- What a great analysis, birds are the only ones who can travel from country to another country without a visa, Us human beings should be able to travel freely just like God intended.
Louverture- Yes yes my dear sister, this poem is great. You are changing our narratives. Listening to this poem is like you, telling my own story of how I freed myself from this jail system and many inmates are doing the same as we speak. We are living our dreams going above and beyond. No inmates are jailbirds anymore; we are all free men and women

who are above and beyond this corrupted system. We are all free to live our full human potentials

Marley- Yes I can relate as well. I did every single thing this society told me to. I graduated at the top of my class, went to college, I graduated with a double major, I even got my masters so I can live the American dream. But instead I found myself in a cage, slaving to this system with a bag of student debt on my back. But I am now a free bird. I have freed myself from this mental slavery. In conclusion I am living my dreams. It's all about me, myself, and I. I matter! My dreams are very important! I am thankful that I have realized my values and I am doing something about it. I am a free bird. I am living my dreams.

Mentor- Yes we are all living our dreams. It's a new era!. It's all about spiritualism. I was inspired by Maya Angelo's poem and found liberation in her literature. I am thankful that I can find a voice in her poem. We have evolved as a people. We are all free like a bird flying in the direction we have chosen to.

Moore- You are right, I understand you Mentor. We all have the right to live where we want to, that's how America was created right? The land of the free, is really the land of prejudice and racism to many of us immigrants and people of color. Everyone knows I've been here for ages and I loved the ideology that you can come from nothing and become a billionaire like Andrew Carnegie or a great intellect like Albert Einstein. It's like our past doesn't define us, whatever you want to achieve you can. Any immigrant can come here and make themselves great while they contribute to the American economy. As all of us knew that was the way of life, until it became clear that the US. President doesn't want us here anymore. That means he doesn't want our money, our ideas, our dreams and in fact our culture in America, land of the free.

Garvey- That is true. We see what is happening in the borders of the United States, we hear of the brutalities of children suffering. We are rich and powerful, and we can't really do anything about it. My question is why? Is it because we are legal in this country now, or because we are not Spanish, or we can't relate?

Castro- I'll answer that question for you; it's because we are immigrants. If we speak, they will say we are trying to overthrow the US government.

Briggs- We need to put order in our own country before we point fingers at an immoral society.

Russwurms- And we will do just that while we ask God to intervene. We all know God answers the prayers of the wounded. God answers the prayers of children. God answers the prayers of anyone who cries out for help. So, let's pray and wait on God's timing. Like we know, his timing is always perfect.

Anakarona- I agree let's give to God our creator the things we cannot change and let's focus on the things we can change. Which is what we have been doing, that is making us millions and creating a better world for us by us!

Angelou- Yes, imagine if many of us didn't have to travel, we all know the luxury of traveling for the sake of traveling we get to learn and grow from one another. But we the diasporas we know and live the misfortune of traveling, where it is wrong for us to be forced to travel, to be forced out of our homes, and separated from our families and loved ones. That's why us, the elite diasporas of this era, we are a powerful group of enlightened immigrants with a great amount of wealth, and skills in this society. We have to be conscious; we are privileged so we must take greater steps not just for ourselves and our families, but for the greater good of humanity worldwide.

Biko- Yes, God made the sun to shine in all parts of the world and oxygen to flow in every mankind's lungs. That means every country in the world has the capacity to flourish evenly and peacefully.

Domingo- Our ancestors came here and made America great by influencing the American people, by creating movements, writing books, singing empowering songs, creating great businesses, showing them sportsmanship and more. But they fail to make their own country a better place and in the process they helped the oppressors create an unbalanced world.

Harrison- They didn't know they were being used to continue Lynch's methods so the white supremacy can continue to flourish.

Mentor- But now we know better and we are exterminating every white supremacy ideology so harmony and peace of mind may thrive

Harrison- Some diasporas are like an adopted child who forgot about their birth mother. Now our adopted mother who never truly loved us wants us out of their home. What must we do sink or swim, you know we will swim, and we will prevail. Or better yet, like Mentor said we must fly like a bird. We are all eagles so let's fly way up knowing that the sky is our beginning. Let's do the impossible, let's move by love, let's be the love and the light for others.

Louverture- America doesn't need another immigrant telling them how to be Americans, but America needs God to touch their souls and heal their wounds. Just like us immigrants need God to help us make ourselves great, to help us make our own countries flourish again.

Biko- It's a new era, and we are tracing the first path of this movement that our great grandchildren will read about in history books. They will understand how we the revolutionaries of our century and made things happen effortlessly without dripping a sweat while we laid back and allowed God to use us as we used our God given talents.

Sengor- Wait what do you mean revolution? I thought we passed that. Come on we smarter human beings now we do not have to fight to solve a problem. All we have to do is talk it out. Have a heart to heart conversation with someone and if we can't, we send blessings of peace and love toward that person. I am against revolution. You see how much blood was shed in the name of revolution? Families got broken up in the name of revolting. People became refugees in the name of revolution and now you want to tell me about some revolutionary group that I definitely don't want to be part of. Since when did the Elite diasporas become a revolutionary party? Because the last time

I checked we are the money team, the doers and makers team.

Gandhi- We are all of that and more.

Ike- we are all about green power.

Sengor- Everyone knows how I feel about revolution. For the ones who are new to our meeting, I lived in refugee camps. In the worst conditions mankind ever lived watching people dying of hunger or from a bullet wound. I was just a child but I always question why us humans couldn't talk things through and live in peace instead of shedding innocent blood. I lost my entire family in the name of revolution. Sorry the world revolution still triggers me; it is no secret I am in therapy because of that. So, what are the benefits of revolting? That's all. I am all about, love, peace and unity.

Biko- Listen my friend I am sorry that you experience those hardships in the name of revolution but we are the dreamers team, the money team, the green power team. We are all about love, peace and unity. But what you and everyone else in our team needs to understand is that every immigrant and their parents are fighting for the American dream. They all want to come here, they want to have their permanent residency in America, they want their children to sound and look like Americans and carry that American passport. But we are the outcasts that are saying "Peace out America! We will see you when we come to visit. Enjoy your beautiful country with your beautiful people. While us immigrants we will leave America in peace to go establish in our lands. Us immigrants can have peace, love, and unity while we enjoy our beautiful countries, prosper in our wonderful lands with our country's inhabitants.

Sengor- Okay, thank you for the clarification. I now understand that we are against the norms. We are revolting by leaving America instead of fighting to stay like many immigrants are fighting to be part of America's melting pot

Biko- Yes that's all we are doing my friend!

Sengor- You know what I agree with you now, you are right Biko we are revolting. We are revolting against the norm; we are revolting against this white supremacy that was controlling us for 400 years.

Biko- Thank you for acknowledging that I am right for the first time. (everyone laughs) now let's continue the meeting

Crosswaith- Thank you Sengor and Biko for the clarification. What I want to say is this. I worked hard and achieved the American dream, I even surpassed it. But I always felt like I didn't belong. The American people always made me feel I was less than them. Then Trump got in office and he made my job extra hard. I was the manager of the company, but everyone made me feel like I was stupid in the office because I was not an American and my accent is thick. They only had the TV in the break room on FOX channel. When I thought my Black American brothers would've backed me up, they only made me feel worse. Throwing shade and talking about how it's the immigrants' fault that the Black Americans can't find jobs. At first, I was mad. I hated my job and I thought they were just jealous because I had my PhD and got promoted while they felt I didn't deserve the position. Then I had the flu so took a couple days off work and I got to analyze the situation. Both the White and the Black Americans were right. There were other people with PhDs in the office who were way better than me. But, the owner of the company only gave me the position because I spoke more than one language and everyone in the office knew that. I put myself in their shoes and I clearly understood their frustration and pain. So, I went back to work, put in a 2 weeks' notice, and left the country. I am not telling any of you to do the same, but I just needed some time off to find myself. I just felt content to be out of America and disconnected myself so I could have proper self-care. When I went back to my country I had time to think, I was out the rat race, running like I was in a marathon for the next train. I was around nature, I was able to meditate and find my true self, my true calling. I started listening to motivational talks again, meaning I had the time for it too. Then God directed me to the video "**Louise Hay I can do it; I accept my power.**" I listened to that same video for 30 days non-stop along with her other videos. And of course, other great speakers who speak on self-love, self-pride, self-richness and anything else I personally needed to grow as a human being. I even did the mirror work where I look at myself in the mirror and say my affirmations. I had work to be done my friends, and I am thankful I did the work. I faced my pain and conquered all my fears. I was insecure and didn't even know it. I was dealing with many generational curses and I had to remove each one of many blockages out of my mind, body and soul before I could be my 100% self.

Then I stumbled on Dr. Joseph Murphy and was able to download his book *The power of the subconscious mind* for free. This intelligent man knows how to break things down for real. I was impressed. There was stuff I never heard before. I understood a lot of things and I also started to change drastically. After that my life became a bundle of joy. I was happy all the time and it was a blessing to be alive at this perfect timing. There is this one affirmation from Louis Hay I used to say to myself all the time and I still do it today. It is, "**I am worthy of the very best in life and I am now lovingly allowing myself to accept it!**" I believe this affirmation opened the door to my richness, my life worth living. I am so thankful that I was able to do my inner work and I believe everyone who wants a better life should do their own inner work, whatever works for them.

Mentor- that is 100 percent true

Crosswaith- yes, listening to different motivational speakers I realized it's not all about me but about us, for our greater good as humanity. Then I ordered *Think and Grow Rich* and the *Master Key to Riches* by Napoleon Hill like Mentor had told me too. Can you believe they delivered them in my country? I was amazed, trust me you will be too if you were me. By the time I left my country, only one person owned a telephone in my town, and everyone used that phone like it was a pay phone. Now I go back and I see I can order things online and have it shipped directly to me. I was amazed. I am telling you I was happy at the smallest things and I was proud of myself for the regular things in life.

Then I started seeing opportunities everywhere I went in my country. Within a month I had a business plan in mind, so I wrote it down in my gratitude journal and I started taking small steps toward it. God put the right people in my life and next thing you know my PhD was well needed in my country. I came back to the United States and took everything out of my savings and went back to my country and invested in my business. Once more money came in from my business, I invested in other businesses. Everything took off and now I am a king like Akon in my own country. You know what, my co-workers from the states were my customers, too. They liked my business pages and shared it. I was shocked, then I realized it was all part of the process; they had to make me feel uncomfortable so I can be who I am today. When I see Trump, I will tell him thank you for making me feel like shit when you called my country a shit hole country. By the grace of God, now I am picking up my shits in my shit hole country that's making me billions. And to the ones that said I was crazy; I'll tell them yes I am a crazy billionaire how about that!

Rodney- Wow that's inspiring. Everyone please give this billionaire a round of applause he deserves to be honored! (everyone stands up and claps)

Crosswaith- Please, please everyone sit down. Please sit down. I am not the one you should clap for. There is no way I could have done all these things by myself. I talk to God every day, I never give up, I keep my faith in my creator. I knew that God had something great in store for me. I am the child of the most high and I believe that I am great just like my creator. I did my affirmations, but I prayed ten times more. I read books after books, but I walked with God 24/7. I work hard in my dreams and visions, but I believe that God is the one who opens all the great doors for me. I know that God is the one that made it possible for me to stand here today to testify to everyone what the God of all gods have done for me. So, don't applaud me but worship him and believe that God is a living God. He is involved and helping us in every step of the way. So, talk to God every day and never give up my brothers and sisters

Everyone- Amen!

Rodney- You are so right, and we will take your advice and walk with God by our side. But you know who you remind me of? Tyler Perry. Everyone knows who he is right? If you don't please Google him because he did the same thing as our friend right here. Tyler Perry said at the BET awards, when everyone was fighting for a seat at the table he was in Atlanta building his own. And you my dear immigrant, when everyone was fighting to live in America to live the American dream, you my friend you went back home and created your own. You also created jobs and a better way of living for everyone in your countries and I know your company will only expand from here. Please let us know if you need any partners to run one in our own country.

Anakarona-. America may not need you but us immigrants, especially Black diaspores, we need each other. Let us know when you are ready to expand your company and I will have a chain in my country, and I know everyone here will agree as well. We have to open big businesses and give people jobs that pays them well, so they don't have to leave our country and come to America by any means necessary. America is full of problems right now. They don't even know what to do with themselves, but they want to blame everything on us immigrants. I don't know about you, but I came here as a child. Just like Andrew Carnegie I didn't make the choice to come here, but the choice was made for me. And now I just don't want to be part of anyone or anyplace who doesn't want me or know my worth. My peace and harmony is more important than a fake, fraud American dream. May the God of love and peace help this nation who once gave dreamers hope. I thank God for all the opportunities America has offered me and for all the great people I got to meet but my time in this precious land is running out. It's not a goodbye, but see you soon because I have businesses in this country as well but I now reside in my own country of birth, too.

Crosswaite- That's a great idea! Multiple strings of income, that's the quickest way to be financially independent! Anyone who thinks my company will be a success in their country please hit me up. Text me and we will expand. Also, if you feel that your company will be good in my country or someone else's country let's talk business. Let's see how we can evolve ourselves and create a legacy and everyone will eat and be merry from each other's companies. You know what that's how it used to be back in my grandparents' day in the village. They all helped each other for free in each other's farm and when it was harvest season everyone had plenty of goods from each other's garden.

Mentor- Yes yes yes! That was the purpose of today's meeting. I wanted us to link up, to expand our ideas worldwide. As we can see the world is getting small again. Everyone here has a phone with Google Translate so let's make magnitudes happen for us and for everyone who's thinking of taking the risk and crossing the borders just to find out that America is no longer taking no refugees.

Louverture- Us doing that is helping the American people as well. They want us out and we are getting out and creating our own just like Tyler Perry.

Gandhi- Yes in that order! A great man by the name of Gandhi once said, "Earth provides enough to satisfy every man's need."

Domingo- Wait, didn't your great-great-great uncle say that?

Gandhi- Yes thank you. I believe Gandhi the great said, "Earth provides enough to satisfy every man's need." So that means not only America provides the needs but the whole earth. Which means every continent, every country, every state, every city, every province provides enough to satisfy every man's needs.

Mentor- I don't even know what to say right now. I'm just happy to see how God has taken full control of this meeting. I applaud that everyone of us is on a higher level and wants nothing but good for the greater good of humanity.

Garvey- This is what happens when we allow our creator to take full control of our lives. Can you imagine what we can do? How many people we can help, how many jobs and opportunities we can create? Just imagine for a minute, let's take a moment of silence and imagine to imagine the great things we really want.

Everyone in the room sits silently with their eyes closed and imagining. Some people were smiling as they began to imagine the goods they wanted out of life, while others had straight faces so they could grasp every little image of their visualization. After ten minutes the timer rings and everyone begins to open their eyes one by one.

Garvey- I feel great! What a great way to end this meeting. Matter of fact I'm like a bird, a great eagle flying high in the sky building his nest wherever in the world I pleases.

Mentor- Wait, before everyone leaves I have a poem I want to leave in your heart.

Garvey- What is this? A poetry slam night? Come on Mentor you know I have a plane to catch

Mentor- 5 minutes Garvey. Trust me my friend you will appreciate it! And everybody in this room needs to hear the voice of my heart.

Garvey- Alright. I am listening

Everyone- Preach Mentor. We are listening with the ears of our heart!

Mentor- (smiles) Thank you everyone!

It's our time!

Everyone- Yes it is, yes it is our time!

It's Our Time!

It's our time to express ourselves.
State how we feel, drop every tea
and own up each block.
It's Our Time!
It's our time to run our own marathon!
Continue the victory without looking back
Until we reach our goals.
It's our Time!
It's our time to create jobs
Bring home the victory
And even change mentalities!
It's our Time!
Every barricade step to the side
we bringing home the victory
It's our Time!
We are the masters of ourselves
We are tracing the first path!
The first path that will bring change
Make us see clear
reflect before we act
And even change this broken system
It's our Time!
To show others what we are made off
To show others who we are
while we start by changing self
Question all truths
And Even unite with the king of kings
It's our Time!
It's our time to let go of every nonsense
and take life seriously
After all

We were not asked to be born
You damn right!
we gots to know
why were we born?
Who created us?
And How the hell did we get here on this earth?
We even have the audacity to ask for the path to
our destiny!
Anyways
It's our time!
Mumbling never does you any good, And
talking trash only brings you pain!
Wants a better life do not walk with hatred
I'll tell you, it's our time!
We have to let go of every pain!
Let's reconstruct love that is dominated with
charity
Collaborated with sensibility of humanity
It's our time!
let's never look back,
while we walk with the divine power
without even questioning the hardship of life
Hmmmm
It's our time!
Today is my turn, tomorrow is yours
It doesn't mean that we have to live a Coup
D'etat!
hmmm
It's our time!
We must remove ourselves from every negative
states
So, we can move to a higher state
Without walking thru a path

That will have us washed out
It's our time!
It's our time to get in the front line
Get uncomfortable
live a life of examples
with the secret fortunes of life
It's our time!
It's my time!
To express myself with modesty
It's our time!
Words from my mouth will give you joy to live
But!
words from your mouth are the source of life
It's our time!
Unity will bring a pleasurable life
It's our time!
If you didn't know that I'll tell you again
It's our time!
My generation stand up firm
Ready to defend a life full of sense
It's our time!

Everyone- encore, encore, encore

Mentor- Thank you everyone. Before we depart the floor is open for anyone to express themselves, through words, poems, or even sing a song of hope. Especially our new members. We would like to add you to our WhatsApp group where we share ideas and also continue this conversation.

Louverture- I know my friend Garvey has to catch a flight, but I just want to mention one thing before we leave. I want all my leaders to remember that this December 2019 that just passed was the year of the return. 2019 marked the 400 years that our ancestors were forced to leave their homes and work for free labor to build up white supremacies empires, economies, infrastructures. Let's make this year the year that we truly go back to where we came from. Wherever in the world we feel comfortable and build up our own empire while we are giving people great labors, sustainable jobs, and great benefits so they can live a meaningful life. So, they can live a great life and they will not have to go to the colonizer's land and get humiliated in cages. We should make this 400 year the year that we start making our ancestors proud, to live our ancestors' wildest dreams and go back home in peace and joy. To end with my message, I will ask each one of you, if not now then when? Remember whatever you ask the universe it will be given to you in plenty. Whatever good you do in the universe and to your brothers and sisters will come back to you. So, let's raise the bar and leave the colonizers' lands like Tyler Perry when people were fighting for a seat at the table he went and built his own! My brothers and sisters, we are bigger and better than this American Dream. We must stop fighting for this American dream and go build our own dreams where we are wanted and needed. Let's go back to our own lands and transform our country's paradigm while we are changing our own paradigms! Who's down with me?

Everyone- Yes yes yes. Let's do it with dignity and grace.

Hughes- But I am African American. I have no desire to go back anywhere. I love America and everything about it. Plus, I am buying blocks after blocks in inner cities in America. I will go visit other countries but, America is my one and only home. I am a native to this land.

Douglas- Then my brother continues to invest, create jobs and make millions in America in your communities

Anakarona- Please do, we want everyone to be successful wherever in the world they feel comfortable and at peace. God has blessed us with free will and a large planet so why limit ourselves? Why think small? We should start to think big and do big things while we are allowing our heart to guide us.

Mentor- My fellow brothers in sisters we are pro America, and we are pro our native countries, but to be clear we are against the **American Dream!** Because this so-called dream is too small and it limits us from living to our full human potential. So that's why we the diasporas, the immigrants, the anchor babies and the dreamers we say **Fuck the American Dream!**

Marley- All of us here are growing, we are all learning and becoming better men and women. If it is in our heart, desires or if it is our destiny to go back to our native land, we will just like Simba did

Hugo- Simba who?

Marley- Simba from the movie "The Lion King", the one who was forced out of his home as a cube but when he became a lion and made peace with his inner self he realized the importance of going back to his kingdom to fulfill his destiny and that's how he became the king of his world.

Voltaire- Everything makes perfect sense. You are all right my friends, just like Simba we were forced out of our home so God can build us. Now we are being pressured to go back home that means God has a bigger plan for us. That is bigger than The American Dream. We just have to believe that all is well by the grace of our creator.

Marley- All is well, so whatever we choose to do or wherever we choose to live remember to listen to your creator and follow your heart and don't worry about a thing man. Every little thing will be alright.

Harrison- Amen to that! The same God who has blessed America is blessing our countries with peace, love, unity, harmony and prosperity. If I missed something please feel free to add it.

Domingo- We want America to prosper but we want to prosper too, why not? There are more than enough in this world for every human being so why not go for it?

Louverture- Plus we know better. We understand what we wish for our neighbor, we also wish it for ourselves. We want good for ourselves. It is important that we want good for everyone else too. Remember before slavery every country in North and South America and the entire continent of Africa were prospering gold and diamonds were all over the ground. They had plenty of fruits and vegetables to share with the rest of the world. The natives were living well, all those countries had more than enough. That was the case hundreds of years ago so it can be the same again. Matter of fact, all those so-called third world countries can be great again. We want for every country to prosper and live to their fullest potentials that's all. We have no malicious feelings toward Americans or any other nations who were built by our ancestors' blood. We are a group of lovers and we only want to project our loves in the universe while we are making billions of dollars.

Hughes- To be honest with you all, now I have a clear understanding of our ideology. Now I feel more comfortable here. It's pretty clear that I am the only true Yankee here, and I have to know where I stand in this group of leaders.

Tubman- No brother, you are not the only Yankee in here. I am your sister from Brooklyn. Born and raised in BK! My great-great-great grandmama was from down south. She was born on the master plantation. Years later she escaped and helped others to free themselves from slavery too. My great granddaddy was a Cherokee Native American, so you know this land is 100% mine. I inherit this massive land. I am a true American and I am proud of my heritage as an African American and Native American. I am American to my core, so you already know how I feel about my land. But what I will say is this. I understand what my Black brothers and sisters from other countries are saying. I am tired of seeing little Black malnourished kids from Africa on T.V and hearing that Haiti is the poorest country in the western hemisphere. It is time people go back home and create jobs for their people. I remember when I was young Jay-Z came to my project, Marcy project giving out air conditioners during the hot summer months. My mother refused to go get one, saying that we are not charity cases.. I was upset as a child, our neighbors said she was too prideful. They were right, but you know what as I got older I understand my mama felt helpless and incapable of doing anything for herself or her children. But I'll tell you what, when Jay-Z opened the Barclay center my mama was one of the first one's who got a job there. That job gives her self-worth and dignity. She felt like she was alive and strong. Today she is one of Barclay's assistant managers in the food court and she is proud to work for a black billionaire. So, the same thing goes for every poor country, city or town. We the black elites it is our duty to go where we are called to and create jobs, give the people something to live for so they can feel like my mama. Let's raise the bar and make the impossible possible for all. We are true entrepreneurs. We have superpowers. We made things happen out of nothing by the grace of the most high, so let's take our entrepreneurship to the very top. I am ready to do businesses outside of America. The U.S. President has hotels everywhere in the world so why not me? Why not expand my empire in the motherland and the Caribbean? I don't want to choose so I'll do it all, why not? I am ready to do businesses and travel to places where people look like me and treat me like I am their family!

Biko- You are right I greatly agree with you, plus most of us immigrants have many businesses in America. we are not abandoning them. we are just expanding to our native countries too. So, my advice to all my Americans is that we love you and we want you to invest in your peoples especially the ones whose ancestors were forced to make America great with free labors. That's the only way America will stand tall in this New Era. We are thankful for America, we love America. My advice to my fellow immigrants, the ones who feel humiliated by the way that America the land of the Free is treating immigrants like ourselves please do not fight to live where you are not wanted but instead find peace within yourself and the Great God will direct your path. The ones who want more than what America has to offer, us the outcast, the thinkers, the dreamers let's expand our wings like eagles. It's our duty to go back and invest in our own native lands. It's our duty to make ourselves great Again!

Mentor- Yes and we will do it with dignity and grace, with peace and joy, while our creator is by our sides every step of the way. We are living our dreams and we are making ourselves great again! We are living our true callings! I love you all equally and have a blessed day. Long live the dream team!

Everyone- Long live the dreamers!

Dessalines- (stands up right after with a trembling voice) Hello Everyone. My name is Jesula Dessalines, in my language my first name means Jesus is here, that means Jesus is present in this great meeting, literally Jesus is here! (everyone laughs) I am new to this group of international billionaires and I am happy that I have manifested everyone in my life, especially my dear friend Dieudonner Louverture who I knew since I first came to America in Junior High School. I would like to personally say thank you to everyone for sharing your knowledge, your inspirational stories, and where you received all of your information. God will bless you and your family for generations and generations to come. But I would like to read a poem to you all before we part ways. Before I do that, I would like to give my number to everyone in this room so I can be part of your great circle of international leaders. I am ready to expand and make money worldwide. It's obvious they don't want us here and I am no coward no sir. I can fight a good fight, but I am wise enough to realize this fight right here, in American soil is not for me. Before I go on my number is (555) 444-1111.Please pay attention as I read my poem. I hope it inspires you all as Mentor's poem has inspired me

Louverture- (whispers) Jesusla, since when you were a poet?

Dessalines- (stands up tall)

I am ready
I am ready to explore the life of wonders!
Liberate myself!
To live my full potential!
Get in touch with my spirituality!
Embrace my physic!
Fall in love with my beautiful soul!
I am ready!
Valuing life is my way of living!
Loving my creator is the air I breathe!
I am leaving in the moment!
Exploring every opportunity!
Living outside my comfort zone is my new thing!
I am ready!
To go beyond my experience!
Valuing the unknown!
Adopting this heroic life!
I am so ready to give it my all!

To transform from who I am to who I was
created to be!
I am ready!
To allow the creator to take full control of my
life!
For the infinite to guide me into my destiny!

Everyone stands up and applauds for Dessalines
Angelou- Beautiful poem, that's your gift from
God. I am proud to say in this room we have
different talents, different professions, different
types of business owners, different languages,
different ways of doing things. I love the fact that
we love and appreciate each other. Plus, each one of

us is doing great things that are adding value to other's lives. That's a blessing from above to belong to a group of wonderful people, world leaders like yourselves. Please give yourselves a round of applause (everyone stands up and claps). This meeting has adjourned. Please take each other's information and continue to raise each other's vibration and make billions of dollars while we are inspiring billions of people in this new era called Spiritualism! I also hope by now everyone has a copy of both books *Think and Grow Rich* by Napoleon Hill and *Psycho-cybernetics* by Maxwell Maltz. The new members in our team, make sure you get a copy online tonight. It's a must read but at your own intellectual paste. Now the meeting is officially adjourned. As we know the same God who brought each one of us here safe will make sure that we all get to our destinations safely.

Everyone- Amen!

As the meeting ended, everyone exchanged numbers, email and social media info, and they hugged each other as they left one by one.

Louverture- Jesusla, wait up. You know I want to talk to you right? I didn't know you wrote poetry, that's amazing!

Jesusla Dessalines- Yes I do Thank you also thank you so much for inviting me to this meeting. Thank you so much for everything. Now I have to rearrange my vision board. (gives Louverture a hug)

Louverture- Make sure you add me in in your vision board, but I am leaving the country tomorrow please come with me

Dessalines- You know I work tomorrow

Louverture- You're my future. With me you don't need that job anymore

Dessalines- Number one I never agreed on being your future wife. And two, it doesn't matter how much money you have. I want to make my own money. I will quit my job at my own terms.

Louverture- Okay I will wait for when you're ready to travel the world with me

Dessalines- I will definitely travel the world with my future husband

Louverture- You know I love you and I know you love me too so please stop playing hard to get. Let's enjoy each other's company and each other's love

Dessalines- Wait, did you even ask me out? (smiling)

Louverture- Really? (laugh) Fair enough, will you please be my girl! Please say yes

Dessalines- Why? Do you want some of my good Karma?

Louverture- Of course, (hug her thigh) please drop them on me baby. I am getting ready to go over your house too, my love. To have a real conversation with your mommy and let her know what are my intentions with my soon to be wife

Dessalines- Dieudonner Toussaint, I hope you are serious. I do not have time for childish games. I'm all about my businesses and influencing the world.

Louverture- (look at Dessalines in the eyes) I know too much to play childish games. I am serious about us and I am deeply in love with you. (grabs Jesusla and tongue kisses her as his hands feel on her shape.) I love you. You will see I mean business pretty soon, but let's go out to lunch and after that we will go to your house so I can speak to your mom before I go to Haiti tomorrow.

Dessalines- Okay, but like they say actions speak louder than words my friend.

Louverture- You mean boyfriend. Cheri, are you coming out to lunch with me?

Dessalines- (smile) You're lucky I'm hungry, let's get out of here. We are the only ones left. (starts walking out the door)

Louverture- Oh, why Haitian women love to play hard to get!

Dessalines- (stops, look backs, points her finger at Toussaint's face) Because Haitian men, love the game and that's what you guys love about us!

Louverture- (licks his lips) you damn right. I love all that sassiness, with your sexy chocolate self! (speed walk to catch up to her and hold her hands) Is that a YES?

Dessalines- (her heart full of passion beating uncontrollably) MAYBE

They hold each other's hands as they walk out the room that was filled with over hundreds of world leaders who will change the world for the better. Each one of them knows that the road they will travel will be easy, because they strongly believe that God, their creator, will guide their path and will walk with them every step of the way as they fulfill their destiny!

Yes, I can!
With faith, yes I can!
Without looking back, yes I can!
My creator is guiding me so it is obvious that I
can
Without any stress I will reach my destination!
walking tranquil I am at ease!
It is my destiny!
my path!
How dare you evaluate what's mine?
When my father told me Yes I can!
My head is held high because I can!
I am living in peace!
You didn't know that I could?
My destiny is writing in my heart
I am rejoicing with my sisters
Enjoying life with my brothers
No need to fear me
Yes, we can!
With my creator's help, yes I can!
All that I want to do, what my 2 eyes can see, and
what I imagine
Yes, I can!
The powers are in my hands, I am on the right
path
Yes it is I that can
They told you I am mysterious because I can?
They call me all types of beautiful names because
I can?
I took on all challenges,
I, a young lady
Who is making you reflect
Relax yes I can!

Oh, you are shocked?
Yes, I can!
My mother trained me so that I can
The creator has created me, he informed me, he
inspired me, to let you know
We can
Yes, we can!
Yes I Can!

About the Author

Lory Mentor is a poet and writer. Born in Haiti and spent her childhood in Haiti where she fell in love with Haitian and French literature. She came to America to reconcile with her mother and became fascinated by immigrants like herself and their journey to the Land of Opportunities. Lory felt like immigrant stories were never told or were rarely documented. Her passion for literature grew stronger and her urge to tell the stories became a quest. Fok, the American Dream is the story of all immigrants from different walks of life.

FOK The American Dream!